Look for More Titles by Cassandra Chandler

LINGERING TOUCH

Other Works
CRAFTING A WRITER'S LIFE: Building a Foundation

Coming Soon

The Blades of Janus
PERIHELION

The Department of Homeworld Security
Nothing to Declare

Homeworld for the Holidays

The Department of Homeworld Security
Book Twelve

Cassandra Chandler

Copyright Page

This book is pure fiction. All characters, places, names, and events are products of the author's imagination or used solely in a fictitious manner. Any resemblance to any people, places, things, or events that have ever existed or will ever exist is entirely coincidental.

Homeworld for the Holidays
The Department of Homeworld Security, Book Twelve
Copyright © 2019 by Cassandra Chandler
Print ISBN: 978-1-945702-46-4
Digital ISBN: 978-1-945702-45-7
Edited by Eliza Sinclair

First eBook edition: December 2019
First print edition: December 2019
10 9 8 7 6 5 4 3 2 1

cassandra-chandler.com
P.O. Box 91
Mission, Kansas 66201

Dedication

For my readers—thank you for joining me on these adventures!

Don't miss out on any of the alien action. Subscribe to Cassandra Chandler's newsletter at cassandra-chandler.com!

Prologue

Summer

"Protocols, protocols." Nika murmured the word under her breath, knowing she was about to seriously break some.

No unauthorized contact with Earthlings. Minimize interactions when she couldn't avoid them.

Nika had already received special permission to join Kyle and Tracey while they visited Tracey's family—all of them Earthlings with no idea that Tracey's new boyfriend was a human-Tau Ceti hybrid, or that their tag-along friend was an alien from Sadr-4.

Using an Earth car for the "road trip" had been incredibly enlightening. Nika had a much better understanding of traffic patterns, how transports were used on Earth, and how to create vehicles that wouldn't stand out from the variety of designs around them.

The trip wasn't over, but under no circumstances should Nika be entering the restaurant connected to the gas station where she and her friends had stopped for fuel. If only the food didn't smell so good.

"Buddy's House of Subs" was painted on the plate glass windows in front of the place, along with a picture of a person riding a long, thin sandwich that appeared to be leaping out of the ocean for some reason.

Nika didn't let herself stop to analyze just how many things were wrong with that picture. The waterlogged bread alone would ruin the sandwich.

She glanced over her shoulder and saw that Kyle and Tracey were still busy. Tracey had her arms around Kyle's shoulders and Kyle had his hands on Tracey's hips. Their foreheads were pressed together as they spoke quietly while the fuel dispenser refilled their car.

Nika felt a little tug in her chest and a heaviness deep in her gut. It seemed like everyone around her was finding a connection that eluded her. Well, except when she was working on her machines.

Apparently, Earthlings were capable of forging connections with anyone. Sadirians like her, Tau Ceti like Kyle and his dad, even Zemanni, the infamous Scorpiian assassin. Everybody was pairbonding.

Nika had taken to considering probabilities around who would pairbond next. Their group's chief medical officer, Dane, was at the top of her list. Nika herself was close to the bottom of it.

Who needed someone to kiss when she had starships to fix and Earth tech to upgrade? Nika even had access to super-advanced Vegan technology—something she'd never dreamed she'd have the opportunity to explore.

There were plenty of other priorities to keep her attention. She snorted, then slipped through the door to the restaurant.

The floor was made of large black and white tiles. A long counter separated the main sitting area and the food preparation facilities. Nika had been in enough Earth establishments to understand how that worked.

Normally, one of the Earthling members of the Department of Homeworld Security would be with her to do the interacting, though. Lucky for her, the place was almost empty.

The smell was stronger inside. Rich and not overly sweet, but definitely not savory. She wanted to just stand there and sniff the air, but knew that would be weird by Earth standards. Instead, she headed to the bar and sat down.

"What can I get for you?" The man behind the counter turned toward her, his voice a deep rumble that made goosebumps rise on her skin.

She rubbed her arm and said, "I'll have—"

The Earth language that had been imprinted into her brain before her assignment to the planet suddenly vanished. She stammered incomprehensibly as she stared into clear gray eyes surrounded by thick, dark lashes. The rest of the man's features registered in quick succession.

He had a strong nose, bent halfway down as if it'd been

broken and hadn't healed right. His hair was dark and wavy —so unruly, she wondered if he'd done more than run his fingers through it after waking.

His lips were fuller than most of the humans' she'd encountered in this area, his skin tanned to a dark gold and embellished with intricate art. The design looked like it had been somehow fused with his skin.

He rested his elbows on the counter, hands folded as he smirked at her. She leaned in, bringing their faces closer together.

"You see anything you like?" he said.

"I... Um..." Words slowly formed. She hoped they were the right ones. "Sandwich. Just... sandwich."

He pulled in a breath through clenched teeth, making a strange sound, and shook his head. "I'm sorry, but we don't serve 'just sandwiches' here. What we do have are subs that will rock your world."

"Rocking." She nodded. "That sounds good."

It sounded better than good. It sounded amazing, especially if she could keep staring at him. There was an open space between where he stood behind the counter and the kitchen area. She hoped she would still be able to see him while he worked.

"You want pickles with that?" His grin deepened.

"Sure."

He leaned back abruptly and yelled, "Pickles!"

The action was strange enough to snap Nika's attention

back to her environment. Engineer or not, she was supposed to be a trained soldier. She suddenly realized she didn't even know what "pickles" were. And that she'd been outright ogling the Earthling.

A clacking sound emanated from behind the counter, like claws on the tile. Something was coming. Nika slid from the barstool, ready to face whatever was heading her way.

A tiny, round ball of reddish fluff scrabbled around the edge of the counter. It had big brown eyes, a pointed muzzle, and lots of sharp teeth. She could see them clearly, because its mouth was open, its tongue hanging out to the side.

Somehow, it seemed like it was laughing at her.

Nika looked over at the man, whose grin had only grown.

"I'm not eating that," she said.

"Of course you aren't. We don't serve hot dogs here."

The creature let out series of percussive sounds in quick succession, then growled at the Earthling.

"Quit barking." The man shook his head. "He doesn't like that joke."

"I'm very confused."

He laughed, the rumbling sound setting off a cascade failure in her brain and melting her innards to slag at the same time. Nika sat back on the stool and planted her hands on the counter, focusing on the planet's gravity, the unrecirculated air with all its smells—anything but the new power source smiling in front of her.

"Sorry," he said, scooting a little closer. "I can't help myself with beautiful strangers."

"Beautiful?"

His full lips pulled into a smirk. Nika folded her hands together to resist the urge to reach out and see how rough his stubble would feel against her palm.

"I bet you get that all the time," he said.

"Not really."

On the ship, she was valued for her skill. Everyone was valued for their skill, not their appearances. Which was good, because most of the soldiers assigned to the *Arbiter* along with her were glitches who had turned out vastly different than the genetic engineers intended.

Honestly, a lot of her crewmates looked more like this guy than a typical Sadirian.

The Earthling arched an eyebrow. "I don't believe that for a second."

"I'm not from around here."

His gaze swept over her arms, then traveled down her torso. He rose up a little higher on his toes so he could keep inspecting her, all the way down to her feet. When he leaned back, his eyes were heavy-lidded, and filled with heat that crackled through the air between them.

"That, I believe," he said. "Let's start over, then. I'm Buddy. That's my dog, Pickles."

He stood and extended his hand in the standard greeting for this area. Nika stared at it briefly before grasping it.

As she'd suspected, the feeling of heat intensified the moment they touched, her skin pebbling, her toes curling, and fire like the energy core of a starship igniting in her belly.

Buddy held on to her hand in silence for longer than the usual Earth custom. He ran his thumb over the back of her hand, his smile muted.

"Welcome to the sub shop," he said, his voice quieter. "I... I hope you're not just passing through."

She realized she'd been holding her breath. She blew it out slowly and nodded, unable to tear her gaze away from his.

"Me, too," she said.

Chapter One

Winter

Everything was perfect.

Buddy stepped onto the sidewalk, surveying the work he'd done in his front yard. Lights twined around the orange tree and hugged the branches. A "Santa and his Reindeer" that was almost life-sized filled most of Buddy's yard, surrounded by other holiday figures. Every edge of the house itself was outlined in multi-colored lights.

He'd skirted close to going overboard, but thought he'd pulled off the right balance. Now he just needed the guest of honor.

On cue, headlights cut across the seashell-and-asphalt road. Nika pulled up in her sleek silver truck, her eyes wide as she stared out the window. The *closed* window.

For such a state-of-the-art vehicle, it never made sense to Buddy that the windows didn't open. Nika had explained once, talking about AC efficiencies and techno-stuff he didn't understand, but what if she wanted fresh air?

The night was chilly, adding a crisp snap to it. At least,

as close to a crisp snap as they could get in Florida. It was one of the few reminders that today was the first day of Winter.

"Get it together, Buddy." He smiled and waved at Nika as she stepped onto the sidewalk, then slowly closed the door behind her.

"Wow," she said. "This is…"

"I wanted to surprise you." He approached, turning to gesture toward his display when he reached her. "What do you think?"

Her eyebrows were high on her forehead. The multicolored lights cast a rainbow glow on her brown skin and reflected off her dark eyes—the warmest eyes he'd ever looked into.

"I think it's a lot of lights," she said.

"Well, it's Christmas. I mean, almost. I don't want to presume about how you celebrate the season, so that's why I invited you over today."

"What's today?"

"The Winter Solstice. I figure, as much as everybody does their own thing, we can all agree that today is the first day of Winter." He quickly added, "In the Northern Hemisphere."

"I didn't know people celebrated that," she said.

"People celebrate all kinds of things. What about you? What's your favorite holiday of the season?"

"I've never actually celebrated anything."

"Wait, like…ever?"

She thought for a moment, then said, "There was that special sub you made me after I fixed your deep freeze. You said that was something to celebrate."

"Yeah, but that's… I'm talking about holidays. You've never celebrated a holiday?"

She shook her head.

"Not Christmas or Hanukkah or Kwanzaa or… anything?" he asked.

She raised her arms slightly, then let them drop back to her sides.

"That's kinda…rough." He ran his hand over the back of his head, ruffling his hair.

"But this is beautiful." She gestured toward his house and took a step closer to him. "I'd like to learn more about it."

Buddy could feel that he was grinning like an idiot, but couldn't stop himself. Nika did that to him. No other woman had ever gotten to him like she did.

He had friends who chose not to celebrate holidays for various reasons, but for them, it was a choice. He'd already figured out that Nika's childhood had been beyond sheltered. She didn't get the simplest expressions, sometimes. It was almost like she was brought up on a different planet. But at least she was trying to broaden her horizons.

"Where do you want to start?" he asked.

She strolled around the Santa, but stopped on the other side of the sleigh and gazed up at Buddy with a questioning look.

Of course, she'd go to the vehicle first. She was a mechanic, and near-obsessed with her job, from what he could tell.

"Old St. Nick," Buddy said. "Good idea."

He walked closer and gestured toward the sleigh. "Santa is popular with the kids. He travels around the world on Christmas Eve, flying in his magic sleigh pulled by these here guys." Buddy patted the closest reindeer on the flank, careful not to knock it over.

"The sleigh... flies," she said.

Buddy nodded. "Uh-huh."

"Not because of an engine, but because it's pulled by animals. Who can presumably also fly."

"That about sums it up. Oh, and Santa delivers presents to all the little girls and boys who have been good that year," he added. "Squeezes down the chimney and puts them under a tree we bring inside and decorate for the occasion."

Nika arced a single eyebrow at him. How could she have not heard of Santa? He had to fix that, to share what he could of the childhood she'd been denied.

"I remember one year, I stayed up till midnight and snuck into our living room to see Santa." Buddy smiled as a wave of nostalgia swept through him. "My dad was putting presents under the Christmas tree. He'd dressed up in the costume and everything. But he couldn't resist the cookies mom and I made, and he had to pull down his beard to eat them. When I saw him, I freaked out. He and mom made me promise not to tell my sisters, but I was wrecked the next day."

Nika's eyes widened again. "You believed the story was true?"

"Sure I did. It was a big part of the magic of my childhood."

"And he's part of this Solstice celebration?"

"Not exactly. He's more tied in with Christmas, which is what my family celebrates. We'll have a big get-together in a couple days at my Aunt Verna's place."

And if he could work up the nerve to ask, Nika would be there as his guest.

"There are so many celebrations and holidays around this time of year," he said. "I didn't know which one you observe—or, I guess, don't observe, so… This…" He shrugged. "This is just for us. You and me, together on the Solstice. A new tradition."

"Oh." Her lips tightened in that way that let him know she was trying not to smile. And failing.

He circled around the sleigh until he was standing right in front of her. Taking her hands in his, he walked backwards, leading her toward the house.

"Come on inside and see the tree," he said.

"The tree that you brought inside your house so the made-up man can put presents under it."

Buddy cocked his head as he nodded. "Well, yeah. But it's so much more than the story. It's the memories you make and being with the people you..." His mouth went dry and he stopped, staring down at her.

Say it, Buddy. Come on now.

He opened his mouth, but all he could manage was, "Care about."

Dammit.

Nika smirked up at him, as if she knew what he'd been trying to say. He sure hoped she did, because at this rate, he'd never be able to say the words.

Normally, he was so smooth around women. They would practically throw themselves at him.

Nika was different. He knew she was into him, but she held herself back. She held herself back from everything, as far as he could tell. Everything except her machines. And maybe his sandwiches.

They'd been hanging out as his sub shop for months now. The more time they spent together, the more he liked her.

And the more he had to lose if he accidentally chased her off.

Aside from his family, he'd never told anyone he loved them. Nika was the first person he'd wanted to. He had all night to work himself up to it.

He angled his head toward the house. "It might not get too cold around these parts, but the humidity makes it go straight to your bones. I have hot cider mulling, and I made us a special dinner."

"You're always cooking for me." She stepped a little closer and interlaced their fingers.

His heart started to race. "I have to make sure you keep coming back, don't I?"

"Buddy, that's not the only reason I visit."

"I know." That goofy grin came back with a vengeance, pinching his cheeks almost. "It's also because of my dog."

She busted out laughing, as he'd hoped.

"Pickles is a big motivator," she said. "But that's not what I meant."

He took a deep breath, even though his chest felt full as they smiled at each other for a quiet moment.

"Listen, Nika." His heart was pounding. Moment of truth time. He could do this. "We've been friends for a while now. I was thinking…maybe we could be—"

Her watch let out a piercing beep.

Something more, he finished in his head.

"I'm sorry," Nika said. "I have to take this."

Buddy sighed and nodded. They'd been through this before.

"I get it," he said. "It's okay."

"Buddy…"

"No, really. I get it. Your work is important."

"So are you." She let out an exasperated grunt as the beeping intensified.

He stepped away and rubbed the back of his neck as she looked at her watch. He wasn't sure where she'd picked it up, but it seemed much more advanced than other smart watches he'd seen—a perfect match for the smartest woman he'd ever met.

"Crap," she said. "They need me at… At the garage. It might not take long. I can try to come back later tonight."

"Yeah?"

"Yeah." She smiled, but her eyes were pinched around the edges. "I want to taste that dinner you made me."

He tried to keep the mood light, to help her feel better. "I knew you were just after my food."

She laughed again, but then shook her head. "I really am sorry."

"It's okay. You do what you have to do."

She nodded, her eyes glittering in the lights. The sight about did him in.

Strong Nika, woman of iron, with tears in her eyes because she didn't want to leave him. A sandwich guy.

She headed to her truck, her head bowed and shoulders hunched forward. Buddy used all his willpower to keep himself from following her. He waved, even though she wasn't looking, then turned and walked into his house instead.

As soon as he was in the door, Pickles came running, the

little dog's claws clacking on the stone tile of the entryway. He barked a few times, then looked up at Buddy.

"Sorry, Pickles. Our special evening got cancelled."

Pickles let out a whine.

"I feel you," Buddy said.

He'd known Nika was a genius ever since she'd fixed his broiler, his sink, and even rewired the lights in his sub shop, all while explaining efficiencies and sustainability in terms way beyond what he could follow. He had no doubt she was doing really important work. But, dammit, she should be able to have a life.

Every time she was called away, he worried about her. When she was focused on a project, she tuned out everything around her. She'd forget to sleep, to eat.

She had stayed at the sub shop once for two days fixing his deep freeze. He was ready to replace it, but she insisted she could make it work. He kept bringing her sandwiches and water, and had to go back to make sure she'd actually eaten. And he'd practically had to twist her arm to get her to take a nap in the back room.

His deep freeze worked like a dream now. Nothing ever had freezer burn, and his electric bill had plummeted. He knew how valuable her skill sets were. But, dammit, no matter how fancy a car shop she worked at, she shouldn't have to worry about being called away in the middle of the night during the holidays.

Buddy really wanted to give her boss a piece of his

mind. The guy was taking advantage of Nika's dedication.

He trudged to the kitchen, where his special meal was laid out on the table in insulated containers. He never knew when Nika would actually arrive, so it had seemed the best option.

The roast smelled mouth-watering when he unsealed the lid, but what did it matter if Nika wasn't there to share it with them?

Buddy leaned against the counter, arms crossed as he glanced around. His gaze settled on a large picnic basket, and an idea took root.

If her boss wouldn't let Nika have a break, Buddy would take the night off to her.

He grabbed the basket and set it on the counter. Faster than he'd ever moved before, he packed up the dinner he'd made for them. He ran to the door, turning off the lights along the way. He set the basket down and loaded up the pockets of his light jacket with his keys, wallet, and phone.

He glanced out the window and saw that Nika's truck was still parked by the curb. He could see her in the driver's seat, having an animated discussion with whoever was on the other end of that call. She didn't look too happy.

I really hope this fixes that.

"Pickles, be good," he shouted.

He grabbed the basket and slipped out the door, making sure it locked behind him. Buddy snuck across his front yard, dodging snowmen and elves and really wishing he'd maybe left the lights on. The weather had been too dry for that to be safe, though. He reached the back of her truck and managed to get inside without making too much noise. If her truck was any indication, she really did work at an upscale garage. He'd never seen a pickup with such a sturdy shell over the bed, or with the kind of latches and locks this one had. Thank God she'd shown him how to work them when they went to pick up parts for the freezer.

Once he was inside, he set down the basket and found a good place to sit, after making sure the door was shut tight behind him.

This would either be the perfect romantic gesture, or land him in the hottest water he could imagine with her. At least, either way, he'd get a chance to tell her boss what he thought of the guy.

Or tell Nika what he thought of *her*.

Buddy leaned against one of the toolboxes built into the side of the truck and whispered, "I could really use a Christmas miracle about now."

Chapter Two

"This has to be a mistake," Nika murmured. "Why do they need me on the *Reckoning*?"

The mining station, she could understand. Even the lunar colony would have made more sense. And heck, she practically lived on *Outreach*—the space station they were constructing. At least, when she wasn't on Earth with Buddy. But the *Reckoning*?

She ran her fingertips over the etchings on the truck's dash, activating the controls that prepared the engine for something a little more involved than traveling over Earth's roads. She checked the status displays for her main systems. Engine, oxygen, artificial gravity, and cloak. She heard the hiss of the hatches sealing.

As the systems powered up, she leaned back and let out a long breath through pursed lips, trying to control her disappointment and anger.

Other Sadirians had lives outside of their work. Other Sadirians had…partners. Bondmates, even. Why couldn't Nika?

"Because you're the best engineer in the fleet," she

mumbled. "Because you're a *soldier*." She emphasized the last word.

It had never felt like a burden before.

But then, there was the unspoken truth that went beyond both of those facts. The one she couldn't voice, but that constantly ran through her mind.

Because you're needed to get the Outreach *space station and the expanded colonies finished throughout the Sol system before more of your people are displaced from this blasted war. All those sentients who don't have homes anymore. They're all counting on you.*

Nika looked out the window. Buddy's house was dark. He had turned off his holiday lights already. He must not think she was coming back.

And why would he?

She knew their time together had been interrupted...a lot. Buddy had made plans before to show her things— share his life with her. It seemed like some emergency or another always pulled her away.

Tonight had been different, though. It had been...more.

He had done all this, tried to share something so special with her. She couldn't help but wonder what else he might have had planned. And yet again, she'd been pulled away.

Her heart felt like it was being crushed.

She had to protect her people. If only she could explain.

Right. Tell him that I'm an alien. That'll really help us take our relationship to the next level.

As soon as she had a chance, she'd send him a message. Apologize. Again.

She wasn't ready to give up. As she turned from the dark house, she hoped that Buddy felt the same way.

Driving away from the curb felt surreal. Leaving one reality and entering another. She wove through the neighborhood, heading outside of town.

Night had fallen, thankfully. Nika drove as quickly as she could to the near-deserted road that wound away from Buddy's sub shop and the highway it was built next to.

As soon as the last streetlight faded behind her and she could only see what her truck's headlights illuminated, she said, "Computer, conduct a sensor sweep for vehicles, life forms, and audio/video signals outside the transport."

The screen on the dashboard of her truck flickered to life, a topographical map of the surrounding area filling it. A few small animals were identified, but nothing that could cause Nika problems.

"Sensor sweep concluded." The computer's flat monotone had become grating since Nika had started visiting Earth. She needed to work up a new program for it that would add some inflection. Maybe let listeners choose a gender they preferred, like the Earthlings did.

"Are we cleared for planetary departure?" Nika said.

"Affirmative."

Nika activated the truck's cloak, her fingers tracing the etchings in a pattern that had become second nature after all these visits to Buddy. Her lights cut out, but an infra-red view of her surroundings filled the windshield and all the windows in the vehicle, letting her see much more than the limited headlamps had.

She tapped a few more controls, and the truck gave a little shimmy as wings extended from the undercarriage. After a quick glance at the sensor screen to double-check that there was no one around, she engaged the thrusters.

"We can't have Earthlings taking note of an invisible truck taking off," she murmured.

The scenery blurred as the thrusters kicked in fully. For a moment, Nika forgot the stupid protocols and stressful missions and even her sadness over having to leave Buddy so abruptly.

This… This was her favorite part of her job.

The truck bounced a bit, giving her stomach a brief feeling of weightlessness, even in the artificial gravity field. Then the ground fell away beneath her and the windshield filled with stars. They became crisper as she neared the edge of the atmosphere.

And then she was through. She was home.

"Oh, Buddy," she whispered. "I wish I could share this with you."

Buddy's Christmas decorations popped into her head. She laughed as she imagined Santa and his sleigh pulled by flying animals traveling through the sky.

Yeah, Buddy would love this. So many stars. Her view

was filled with them. Everywhere she looked.

She gave herself a moment, letting the pin-pricks of light soothe her spirit. But then, her thoughts shifted to the planets surrounding a good portion of those stars. Planets filled with sentients who needed help.

"Just give me time," she said.

All she needed was time.

If they could hold on a little longer, more lunar colonies could be finished in the Sol system for sentients similar to Sadirians like her. And for those with different physical needs, she'd already begun working on plans for homes on several other celestial bodies in Earth's solar system.

Titan would be a great home for the sentients who thrived in colder temperatures, and she couldn't wait to start terraforming Mars.

So many life forms were looking to the Coalition for help. And the Coalition was looking to *her*.

Some of the sentients would want to stay on their homeworlds. She would work with them, too. Come up with ways to improve their living conditions—if it was safe for them to stay.

That was the worst part of it all. She didn't know how to create defenses against the Tau Centauran Assembly.

Only the Vegans could match their tech level, and the Vegans now called Earth their home. The more inviting Nika could make the Sol system, the better it would be for everyone. They needed to come *here*.

She traced more etchings on the dash, plotting a course that would take her past the *Kindred* colony and the mining stations. The shuttle—because it was only a truck when she was on Earth—turned toward the moon.

Out here, the lunar light was so bright, it was almost hard to look at. Nika stared at it anyway, her heart and mind filling with wonder once more.

"So beautiful…"

Her shuttle passed over to the far side of the moon, out of sight from Earth and into the disruption field her people were generating that blocked any of the Earthlings' orbiting satellites from seeing their new neighbors from the Coalition of Planets.

Thank the stars the Department of Homeworld Security had given the Coalition authorization to settle here. If they hadn't, Nika wasn't sure what would have become of her people.

She stared out the viewports, craning her neck as she passed the mining station in the Van da Graaff crater. Two clear domes criss-crossed with triangular substructures sat on the connected circles that made up the crater. Each dome covered a spire that sank down into the moon and housed their operations.

While building it, the Vegans had insisted they use precious resources to make the living quarters within each spire spacious and comfortable. From the outside, the structures were made of a dark metal dotted with lights from viewports or elevator cars. Inside, there were plants everywhere, stone fountains made to look like natural waterfalls, and hallways and chambers that took up an exorbitant amount of space.

Honestly, it had taken Nika and most of the other Sadirians a long time to adjust to the design. They were used to living in such cramped quarters—little more than plain metal boxes with regen beds and storage lockers for their spare uniforms.

At first, it had seemed like a ridiculous waste of what could be put to better use. But seeing the smiles on her fellow soldiers' faces, and feeling the sense of ease that was so unlike anything they'd experienced before, she had to admit it was a worthwhile investment.

She turned back to the front viewport, her heartbeat picking up as the *Kindred* colony came into view. Stars, how she loved seeing this.

Even with its special features, the mining station was utilitarian compared to their colony in the Leibnitz crater.

Lush green reached toward the panes of transparent polymer that made up the dome protecting *Kindred* from the moon's lack of atmosphere. White and brown buildings filled the space, while somehow not making it feel crowded. The streets were made of cobblestones and the largest public buildings were wrapped in dirt tunnels to give the Antareans a feeling of home. Plants grew from their tunnels, providing food and oxygen for the colony.

There were rumors that the Vegans were beginning work on terraforming the lunar body. Nika loved to imagine walking on the moon's surface beneath a blue sky. It could easily be as beautiful as Earth.

But the Earthlings would probably notice if their moon suddenly became a lush, green paradise floating above them. That was why work on terraforming Mars had been delayed as well.

Nika let out a little laugh, and wished again that Buddy was there to see this with her. He would love it—once he was over the initial freak-out of discovering that aliens were real. And that she was one of them.

Her smile faded.

Would he get over it, though? She was making a pretty big assumption that he'd accept her as she was.

Just because half a dozen or so Earthlings had fallen for Sadirians or other aliens, that didn't mean Buddy would feel the same. She wasn't even certain he was interested in something more than friendship with her.

The shuttle rose away from the moon, headed toward *Outreach* and the battleship that hovered near it—the *Reckoning*.

The old way and the new, coexisting. Both necessary, especially with the war.

Once the station was completed, they would use it to meet with leaders of worlds that had been brought into the Coalition of Planets, but never given a voice. They would start to fix the wrongs that the High Council had done.

As she headed toward the giant ship, a feeling of dread crept into her. She held on desperately to the glimmer of hope that had sparked to life the moment she met Buddy. She would fix whatever was broken on the *Reckoning* and be back with Buddy in no time.

"This is a new beginning," she said. "It has to be."

Chapter Three

The drive gave Buddy a chance to have second thoughts about his plan. And third thoughts. And fourth thoughts.

But he was locked into it—unless he wanted to throw himself out the back of a moving truck.

He knew he and Nika could have something special together. They just needed to give it a chance. He wouldn't give up on her.

The vibration of the engine stopped. It was the only clue he had that maybe they'd reached their destination. The ride had been so smooth. What the heck kind of suspension did this truck have?

He didn't want to wait too long, and not just because he was tired of sitting in the dark back of the truck. He felt around for the handle and carefully opened the door, slipping out with his basket in hand.

The basket felt heavier than he expected, but as he looked around, that became the least of his worries.

The walls of the garage he was in were white, and looked at least seven stories high. The gray metal floor stretched out bigger than a football field. Bigger than *five* football fields.

And the things parked on that floor...

They weren't cars. They were ships.

Giant ships. Small ships. Medium-sized ships.

*Space*ships.

Some looked like the flying-saucer type spaceships he'd seen in B-sci-fi movies growing up. Others were boxy shuttles, he'd guess.

And then there was Nika's truck, parked against one wall, the light gleaming off its shiny silver sidepanels.

He turned around in a circle, his brain having trouble processing everything he was seeing in the harsh, bright lights. Everything except Nika.

She was standing in front of a large window, staring at... at...

Buddy walked up next to her, his heart pounding in his chest.

Earth. He was staring down at Earth. From the moon— or right next to it, anyway. He could see a curve of the bright white surface in the left corner of the window.

I'm in outer space.

His planet was so much more beautiful than he expected. The blue of the oceans practically glowed against the dark backdrop of space, white clouds swirling over water and land in amazing patterns.

"Whoa, that's really something," he said.

Nika turned toward him. She stared for a moment, then

her eyes widened, her mouth dropping open.

"Buddy?" she gasped.

He nodded, eyes stuck on the window.

"So, um…" He swallowed hard. "I'm guessing you don't actually work on cars."

She grabbed his elbow and pulled him over to the truck and out of sight of the main area.

"What are you doing here?" she said.

"I wanted to surprise you. I brought dinner." He held up the basket and opened the top flap.

Instead of seeing the dishes he'd hastily put in the basket, all he saw was orange fluff. Orange fluff that stretched and turned his head toward them, blinking sleepily.

"You brought your *dog*?" Nika paused after each word, incredulous.

"Not on purpose," Buddy said. "He must have climbed in there when he smelled the food."

"Buddy," Nika said, her grip on his elbow tightening. "You can't be here."

He nodded, looking around again. "Yeah. Yeah, I get that."

"Buddy…" She pinched her eyes shut and lowered her head.

"Hey, you don't have to worry about me telling anybody that…"

His brain seemed to stop, not wanting to see what was

right in front of him. What had been right in front of him the whole time.

Who didn't know about Santa? And sandwiches and seashells and...*bread*?

There were any number of things Nika had been completely clueless about, and Buddy had just thought it was because she'd been sheltered in her childhood. But nobody could not-know that much stuff.

Nobody from Earth.

"I won't tell anyone that you're..." He shook his head. "You know. An alien. Cause I'm guessing that's what you are."

She didn't say anything.

Damn, that cinched it.

An alien. He was in love with an alien.

He ran his palm over his face, then realized his hand was shaking. He had to keep it together. But he was stuck on a spaceship. With his dog, of all things.

"We can hide out till you can take us back," he said. "I don't want you to get in trouble."

"I'm not worried about me." She stepped closer, staring up at him with those gorgeous dark eyes. "If they find you here, they'll erase your memory."

He shrugged, trying to keep his growing panic at bay. "That's not so bad. I can make dinner for you all over again. Maybe not get interrupted this time."

"If they find you on board, they'll erase *all* your

memories of me. All of them."

"What? No. No, that's not right." He took a step back, but the truck blocked him. The truck that was actually a spaceship.

He shook his head. "You guys are the good guys, right? I mean, you're one of them."

"It's our law," she said.

"Nika…" He let out a breath that felt like it emptied him. "I don't want to forget you."

Her lips tightened. She turned back to the window.

"We're going to figure this out," she said. "I can set the autopilot on my truck to take you home."

The blue sphere started to shrink. It took Buddy a minute to realize they had started moving away from it. More and more of the window became filled with blackness and stars.

His heart was pounding and his mouth went dry. Where were they going?

"That doesn't seem good," he said.

"No, no, no." She ran up to the window. Earth was just a tiny speck, and then Buddy lost it among all the other points of light.

"We're still close enough to the Sol system," she said. "I can—"

She sucked in a breath as the stars outside were replaced with a milky blue…something. The colors swirled and eddied, then started to float past the ship faster and faster.

"Blue space," she whispered. "We just dropped into blue space."

"I'm guessing that's bad."

Nika didn't answer. She just kept staring out the window.

"Nika." He gently gripped her elbow. "What does that mean?"

She turned back to him, her eyes wide and...scared.

Aw, hell...

"It means we've left Earth's solar system," she said. "And I don't know where we're going or why."

"Damn," Buddy said. "That *is* bad."

"We have to hide you."

Pickles let out a little whimper.

"Both of you," Nika said.

"Yeah. Hiding sounds good." He ran his hand over his face, letting out a deep breath to try to calm himself. His heart felt like it was going to burst, it was pounding so hard.

Nika started leading him through the maze of ships.

"Wait... We have to hide Pickles, too?" he said, as he followed. "They wouldn't wipe his memory. I mean, he's just a dog."

"No, they will not mind-wipe your dog." She shook her head. "I need to get to engineering and figure out what's going on."

"Sounds like we're in a sci-fi TV show," he murmured.

Nika stopped so fast, he almost ran into her. She wheeled around and grabbed his arm, squeezing hard.

"This is not a game," she said. "This is not a TV show or a fantasy. This is real. My people are at war. If we dropped into blue space, that means we have a mission important enough to take the *Reckoning* away from Earth."

"The *Reckoning*?"

"It's the name of the ship we're on. The *warship*." She paused and let out a little breath. "Buddy… I need you to be safe. Please, you have to do exactly what I say."

"Yeah. Yeah, sure. I'll help however I can." He reached up to cup her cheek. "I never meant for this to happen. I'd never cause you grief, Nika."

"I know, it's just—"

"Nika, you are back!"

Someone spoke behind him. The voice had a strange echo to it that didn't seem to match the big room they were in.

Nika's eyes opened wider than Buddy had ever seen as she looked past him. She grabbed his arms in a vice-like grip.

Crap, we must be busted.

"Sister," Nika said. "Yes, I'm back."

"Sister?"

This was great. Was Buddy going to get a chance to meet Nika's family? Surely they would help. Maybe some good could come of this after all.

When he tried to turn around, Nika's fingers dug into his biceps.

"Ow," he said.

"You are injuring your…" Nika's sister began. "Oh."

"Sister," Nika repeated, her head tilted and a look of near anguish on her face. Somehow, she made the word into a plea.

What the hell was going on?

"You know, I believe I am needed in…the docking bay." The weird echo to her sister's voice intensified the faster she spoke. There were weird clicks mixed in as well. "I look forward to catching up with you at a later time, and in fact will pretend that I did not even see you until that moment. To make it all the more special."

This was their chance to get some help. Did Nika not want him to meet her family or something?

Nika relaxed her grip, letting out a breath. So, they weren't busted after all.

Finally free of Nika's hold, Buddy turned around to thank Nika's sister—and found himself face-to-face with a giant ant.

Like bigger than giant. Like *people-sized* giant.

Its head was the size of a large watermelon, with huge segmented eyes that were strobing different colors. It had so many legs. Most were folded at its sides, but two sets were held in front of its body—easily ready to reach out and grab him.

The welcoming smile he'd felt on his face froze as a wave of panic swept through him, blasting all the way to his fingers and toes. He screamed and backed toward Nika, keeping her behind him.

"Buddy, stop," Nika yelled.

The giant ant jerked back, eyes shining bright yellow and antennae stiffening like lightning rods on top of her head. Her antennae lowered as she shook her head and muttered, "This again?"

Giant ant. Giant ant. What do I do about the giant ant?

"Buddy." Nika was tugging on his arm.

He grabbed her and pulled her against his side. He had to keep her safe, but what could he use as a weapon? All he had was his picnic basket.

Wait, ants loved picnic baskets... Right?

He held it out to the ant-person, stretching his arm as far as he could to keep his distance, and said, "Here. Take it."

"I... Thank you?" The ant-person took the basket from him. Its eyes had settled into a cool green glow and its voice... Its voice was the same one that had been talking to Nika a moment before.

This is the thing Nika calls 'sister'?

Buddy turned to Nika and said, "You're an ant-person?"

"What?" She scowled at him, jerking away from his side. "No, I'm not an ant-person. Antarean." She nodded toward the giant ant. "Sorry."

"*Ant*arean?" he said. "Seriously?"

"It's a weird coincidence," Nika said.

"Most certainly," the ant agreed.

Buddy shook his head. "Why'd you call her 'sister', then?"

"That is my name," the ant—Antarean—said. "You may call me Sister as well. And Nika called you Buddy... Wait, you are Buddy?"

Sister's antennae went straight again, though not quite as stiff as before. Her eyes strobed between white, blue, and green.

"Buddy of the sandwich shop?" Sister said.

"You've heard of me?" He couldn't believe a hit of pride made it through the soul-deep fear he'd been feeling a moment before.

"Of course I have," Sister said. "Your mushroom and vegetable sandwich is second only to the Queen's royal nectar."

"I take it that's a good thing." He managed a lop-sided smile.

This whole situation was so weird. It was almost like a dream, but way too vivid for him to be sleeping.

"Are there sandwiches in this container?" Sister lifted the basket with one set of arms while opening the lid with another.

Pickles jumped up, barking wildly.

"Oh, no," Buddy said. "Pickles!"

"SCREEEEEEEEEE!"

Sister dropped the basket, emitting an ear-piercing shriek. Buddy dashed forward to catch it, keeping Pickles safe.

The Antarean's dozen or so arms flailed wildly as her antennae went rigid again and her eyes glowed yellow, flashlight-bright. She leapt straight up in the air, landing on the underside of the huge flying-saucer style ship above them—and sticking there.

"Aw, man, I'm so sorry about that." Buddy looked up at Sister and said, "You can come down. Pickles won't hurt you."

"What is that thing?" Sister said.

"He's a dog." Buddy laughed as the last of his fear rolled away.

A minute ago, he'd been terrified of this giant ant-person. Now, he wanted to reassure her so she'd stop being afraid of his teeny dog.

Buddy picked Pickles up out of the basket, holding onto his wriggly body with some difficulty. The dog licked Buddy's chin and whined.

"I know, little guy," Buddy said. "I know. But this is Nika's friend. Can you be nice to her?"

"Does it—he—understand you?" Sister asked.

Buddy shrugged. "Some days he seems to understand more than others. I mean, he's a dog, so he's not that smart. Like thinking he could take on a giant ant...arean." He cleared his throat to cover for his slip.

Sister dropped down to the floor again. Her eyes were a dull yellow.

"You don't have dogs where you're from?" Buddy asked.

She shook her head.

He looked over at Nika, remembering how she'd also acted like she didn't know what Pickles was the first time she'd seem him.

"You either?" he said, his voice quiet.

Nika shook her head. "We don't have a lot of things you have…on Earth."

'On Earth.' There it was. Absolutely impossible, yet plain as day, all around him.

This wasn't a dream. It wasn't a nightmare. It was a situation Buddy never, ever thought he'd be anywhere near.

Making alien contact on a spaceship traveling who the heck knew where. Just him and his dog, representing Earth. And still trying to win the heart of the most amazing woman—alien—that he'd ever met.

Chapter Four

Nika had never been more grateful that her were quarters deep in the belly of the ship—near engineering and the main hangar bay. She managed to get Buddy and Pickles to her berth on the *Reckoning* without running into anyone else.

The moment the door shut behind them, she ran to her storage locker and grabbed the uniform she kept there. She sat on her cot and pulled off her boots, throwing them into a corner.

"They'll expect me in engineering." She stood again, tearing off her jacket and tossing it onto the growing pile of her Earth clothes. She grabbed her shirt and pulled it over her head.

"Whoa, whoa," Buddy said. He held up his free hand as if warding her off, looking at the ceiling and the walls. His gaze always seemed to be drawn back to her, though.

If only they had time to explore that...

"Nudity isn't taboo in my culture," she said. "And I'm not stripping completely. But you should face the wall if that'll make you more comfortable."

His face turned bright red. He slowly spun around as she slipped out of her pants, leaving her in the plain black undergarments that all Sadirian soldiers wore.

She grabbed her uniform and pulled it on, snapping the seals of her boots, belt, and collar into place. Her bracer powered on, and she quickly ran a diagnostic to make sure all of her uniform's systems were working as they should.

Buddy was shifting uncomfortably from one foot to another. He tugged at the waistband of his jeans and let out a tense breath.

I really, really wish we had time to explore this.

"You can turn around now," she said.

Buddy's eyes widened as he saw her in her uniform for the first time. His eyebrows rose up his forehead and his lips quirked into a smile.

"I know, I know," she said. "I look like something from a 1950's sci-fi movie."

"That's… Yeah. That's some silver catsuit you have going on."

He actually laughed. The tightness in her chest eased a bit.

"I noticed some flying saucers in that hangar bay," Buddy said.

"Those are interceptors. We use them for small skirmishes within atmospheres."

"Skirmishes, huh?"

"They're rare," she said. "At least, they used to be."

She pulled her hair back with a stretchy band, trying to keep the curls out of her eyes. It didn't seem right to leave Buddy like this, but she had to.

"I don't know what's going on," she said, "but it has to be urgent for me to be called away from my work in your home system."

"Like all those other times you had to leave suddenly."

He didn't seem angry or upset, but she still felt a surge of guilt from his words. She finally had a chance to explain, to help him understand why she kept having to leave.

"I'm designing colonies in the Sol system," she said. "Dome worlds and space stations. Self-contained subterranean habitats on the outer planets and moons. I'm responsible for creating homes for people who have nowhere else to go. For *my* people."

"Your people who do the mind-wipe thing."

"That is nothing compared to the Tau Centauran Assembly."

"The who?"

"Our enemies." Nika stepped up to Buddy and took his hands in hers. "Buddy, my people are at war. And…it's not going well."

She debated how much to tell him. She didn't want to scare him unnecessarily, but she had no idea what they were flying into.

"The fact that my commander, Marq, pulled me from my work in your system means that this mission is vital to my people's survival."

"Okay." Buddy nodded, clearly working to process her words. "What about Earth?"

"Earth is safe," she said.

He let out a little laugh and shook his head. "If you're not safe, with all this fancy technology, how is Earth safe?"

"Earth has been colonized by sentients from the Vega system, and they won't let anything happen to your shared homeworld."

His eyebrows hiked up again. "There are aliens living on Earth now?"

"Lots of them, actually. The Vegans are the only ones who have officially claimed Earth as their home."

"Do they look like us, too? Like you do?"

"No. The Vegans are small, reptilian life forms."

"Lizard people?" He briefly looked away, shaking his head. "Lizard people."

"There are a few other sentients on Earth that don't look human, but most are Sadirians, like me."

"Like you." He let out a forced laugh, dropping his gaze from hers for a few moments. "I'm guessing our governments are keeping this all hush-hush."

"Your governments don't know," she said. "We've been working with a group of Earthlings who formed a first contact committee. They call themselves the Department of Homeworld Security. And they're doing good work. They're part of the reason the Vegans now live on Earth.

They've allowed my people to build colonies in your solar system so that we have a place to call home."

"How's that going to protect us if you're doing poorly in the war?"

His words stung. She started to pull away, but he tightened his grip on her hands and stepped closer.

"I want you to have a home," he said. "I'm glad we can help. But this is all pretty damn terrifying."

"I understand. But Earth is safe. The Vegans actually designed all of the technology you see around you. They gave it to us millennia ago. My people have just been replicating it, but the Vegans have continued to make improvements. As advanced as the Tau Centauran Assembly's technology is, it still can't beat the Vegans'."

"Okay." Buddy nodded, his eyes unfocused. "So having the Vegans on your side is a good thing."

"They're not on my side. They're on Earth's side. And that's just as it should be."

"But if we're helping you, surely they are, too."

"To a point. Earth is their priority, though."

"This is… This is a lot. I mean, to think that I might have been serving sandwiches to aliens without even knowing it." He laughed and smiled at her. A real smile. "I guess I have been, since you're one of my best customers."

Nika smiled back and nodded. "Your sandwiches are really popular."

"That's why you kept doing all those huge orders. I

thought you just had a hungry crew. You know. At the car-garage I thought you worked at."

She couldn't believe her relief that he was still standing near her, still holding her hand and smiling.

"I'll do everything I can to keep you safe during our mission," she said.

"Ah, crap." He let go of her hands and covered his face, then ran his fingers through his hair, making it a tousled mess. "I'm going to miss Christmas, aren't I?"

Nika took in a breath that seemed to stick in her lungs. She nodded.

Buddy shrugged and cast a lopsided smile at her. "I'll manage. But if we can get a message to my family, I'd appreciate it. I don't want them to worry."

"I'll do what I can. In the meantime, stay here with Pickles."

At the mention of his name, Pickles ran over and started jumping up next to Nika's leg, bouncing off of her in his attempts to get attention. He started barking as well.

"Hey, knock it off." Buddy reached down and picked Pickles up, quieting the dog. "We don't want to get caught."

"My chambers are sound-proofed," Nika said. "Not everyone on board shares my taste in Earth music."

"Not everyone on *Earth* shares your taste in Earth music."

She half-smiled at him, unable to manage more. There

was so much at stake here. The fact that Buddy could still make jokes with her was a comfort she would hold onto as she walked into…whatever was going on.

"Don't open the door for anyone," she said.

Buddy laughed. "I wouldn't know how to open it even if I wanted to."

She reached up and rested her hand on his cheek. His stubble prickled against her palm.

Buddy's smile faded. "You will be back, right? I don't like the idea of us being trapped in here."

"I will," she said. "As soon as I can. This is probably a routine mission to check on some of our colonies or to bring survivors to the Sol system."

"Survivors?" His brow creased. "It really is that bad…"

"I'll explain more as soon as I can. Just please, promise me you'll stay here till I get back."

He nodded. "I promise."

She pressed the control pattern that opened the door to her quarters, heart pounding in her throat. Buddy called out to her before she could leave.

"Nika," he said. "For what it's worth… I'm sorry."

She closed her eyes, grateful her back was to him.

How could she blame him for this when she was the one who'd been deceiving him all along? This was her fault. She would find a way to make it right.

She took in a deep, steadying breath, then turned to face him "I'm sorry, too." She forced a smile she knew he'd see right through. No one could read her like he could. "We'll figure this out. That's my promise to you."

Buddy managed a smile as he nodded, but she could see the strain in it. She stepped backwards into the hall and watched the door slide shut. Before she could will herself to action, the communications channel beeped on her uniform.

"Nika, could you join us in the briefing room?" Sorca's voice was smooth as silk over the comms—as always. Nothing flustered the Cygnian hybrid.

Nika's heart immediately started a frantic beat, as if it had kicked on full thrusters. Sorca was head of security on the *Reckoning*. She and Nika were friends, but if Sorca had found out about Buddy, she'd have to report it to their commander.

"I thought I'd be needed in engineering." Nika hurried toward the lift.

"In due time." Sorca ended the transmission with no further explanation.

Nika's thoughts were spinning in circles by the time she exited the lift on the main command level. She headed for the briefing room, her heart in her throat.

Chapter Five

"What the heck have I gotten us into?"

Buddy sat on Nika's cot with Pickles on his lap. The Pomeranian had managed to fall asleep right after Nika left.

Buddy wasn't sure he'd ever sleep again.

"So, aliens are real and living on Earth." He let out a little laugh. "And apparently they like my sandwiches. Who would have thought?"

Pickles whimpered in his sleep. Buddy petted him lightly, just enough to reassure the dog without waking him up.

"It's going to be okay, Pickles." Buddy rested his head against the metal wall. "I sure hope so, anyway."

The door started to open. Buddy leaned forward, expecting to see Nika. But she'd only just left. It seemed too soon for her to be back.

After barely opening three inches, the door closed again. Movement caught his attention down near the floor. A calico kitten charged into the center of the room, then stopped suddenly.

She had big patches of orange and black on an otherwise

white coat. Her ears were flattened as she cocked her head to the side, then looked around.

When her gold eyes landed on Buddy, they widened in a surprise that set the hairs on the back of his neck on end. Something about her expression struck him as eerily human-like.

The kitten bristled, her fur standing on end as her back arched and her tail curled. She turned sideways and bounced away from him several feet.

Okay, that *was more normal.*

"Hey there, girl," Buddy said. "I'm not going to hurt you."

The kitten tilted her head again, as if considering his words. Hell, for all he knew, this was one of those not-human-looking aliens Nika had mentioned earlier. There were lizard people running around, for crying out loud.

"Do you have a name?" Buddy asked, keeping his voice as gentle as he could. "You want to tell me your name?"

The kitten lowered her head, sniffing the floor near Buddy.

"I bet your name is Fluffy," Buddy said.

The kitten narrowed her eyes and let out a little breath through her nose.

Now we're back to weird.

"Okay… Not Fluffy. How about Whiskers?"

She turned around and sat down. Her ears flattened again, but her fur was settling down. She kept her head at an angle so she could look at him from the corner of her eye over her shoulder.

"I never knew a cat could throw shade that well." Buddy shifted a bit, trying to think of a better guess.

The kitten started licking her back, then staring at him, then licking her back, then staring at him.

"You're trying to give me a clue," Buddy said. He looked at her back, with its big swaths of color.

"Patches! Your name is Patches."

The kitten turned back to face him, her tail whipping back and forth in the air. He swore she was smiling at him.

"Wow," he said.

He had to be imagining things. Right?

Just to be safe, he said, "It's nice to meet you, Patches. My name's Buddy. This here is Pickles."

He lifted his hand so Patches could see the sleeping dog. Her eyes widened even more than when she'd first come in, her pupils growing to nearly fill her irises.

"It's okay. This is my dog. He's just an Earth dog, so he's not that smart. I mean, he's smart for a dog, but not like... Like a...space cat, I guess." Buddy shook his head. "What the hell am I doing? Talking to a cat like it can understand me."

The kitten let out a long meow.

Buddy froze. He and Patches stared at each other for a few long moments.

"*Can* you understand me?"

Pickles rustled on Buddy's lap, letting out a huge yawn. The dog looked around, sniffing the air.

"Pickles, you be a good boy," Buddy said. "We have a new friend here."

The kitten's ears perked forward as her eyes locked on Pickles.

"Pickles loves cats," Buddy said. "You guys are closer to his size, so he has a blast playing with you. My mom has two tabbies that like to gang up on him. He can be a little rough, too, though."

Patches lowered her chin till it brushed the floor. Her back end rose up in the air and started wiggling back and forth. Buddy had seen that before too many times to mistake it. An invitation to play.

"Here we go."

Pickles got the message, too. He leapt off of Buddy's lap the moment he saw Patches. He ran over to her, jumping forward and backward and barking.

"Pickles, settle down." Buddy stood and picked up the dog, but Pickles kept barking. "I know the room's supposed to be sound-proofed, but let's not risk it."

Patches started meowing.

"Oh, come on. You, too?"

The kitten ran up to Buddy and walked around his legs in circles. Pickles was squirming like crazy, trying to get down. Buddy let out an exasperated sigh.

With a high, squeaky meow, Patches stretched up and

batted her paws at Buddy's leg, her claws catching in his jeans.

"Can you watch the claws?" Buddy said.

Patches paused for a moment, then retracted her claws.

Holy crap, she can *understand me.*

"Here goes nothing."

He bent down to let Pickles go. The moment his paws touched the floor, Pickles ran toward Patches. The kitten's eyes went wide again, and she jumped up to the closest spot that was out of reach—a six-foot long, four-foot high boxy-looking thing that jutted three feet out from the wall. It was covered with a shiny silver tarp.

Pickles ran over to it and started jumping up and bouncing off it, trying to reach Patches. His claws caught in the tarp, pulling it to the floor. Patches scrambled to stay on her perch.

"Pickles, stop it."

Buddy grabbed the cloth and stood, thinking to throw it back over the box, but paused. A large, curved window made up most of the top of the compartment. It had a padded interior covered in white fabric and even a little neck-pillow for support.

He looked over at the simple cot that was nothing more than thick fabric stretched between metal supports. There were blankets and a pillow on it that looked distinctly Earth-like, crumpled and...non-uniform. But if Nika had this cushy bed, why was there a cot in her room?

More questions for whenever Nika had time.

He nodded toward Patches, who was also staring through the clear lid. "Get down from there."

She let out another little huff of breath, then walked along the lid and leapt over onto the cot. Pickles followed her, a bit more subdued, finally.

Buddy threw the cloth back over the metal and plush bed, then walked over to the cot and sat beside the kitten. He picked up Pickles and held him still while the dog and Patches sniffed each other's noses.

"If you guys are going to play together, you have to play nice," he said. "And don't mess up Nika's room. Got it?"

Patches rose up on her haunches and placed a paw on Buddy's arm. Pickles was panting, his mouth opened in a wide smile and tongue lolling to the side.

"I guess that's as good as I'm going to get." He scratched behind Pickles's ears.

Patches started batting at his hand.

"What, you want me to pet you, too?"

She let out a little meow.

"Okay, then." Buddy rubbed the back of Patches's ears while Pickles curled up next to him. "Looks like it's just us three."

Chapter Six

The briefing room was crowded when Nika arrived. Sorca stood near the door, arms crossed over her chest and cocky smile firmly in place. Her dark brown hair was held up in a tight bun, and her piercing gray eyes gleamed next to her gold skin.

Sorca's bondmate, Eric Peterson, stood across the room on the other side of the compact meeting table that dominated the space. As soon as Nika entered, Eric broke off his conversation with Marq, commander of the *Reckoning*.

Nika hadn't noticed quite how the men contrasted each other until seeing them standing close. Eric had dark hair and eyes. His skin was weathered from exposure to the elements and sunlight of Earth. Marq had blond hair and blue eyes, and his skin was almost unnaturally pale in contrast—the mark of a lifetime aboard ships and stations.

Their heights and builds were the same. Tall and thick, but not quite as muscular as Buddy. Their features were also less rough-hewn. Buddy had laugh-lines around his eyes and mouth. He always seemed to be smiling.

Except all those times I left him, like just now…

"Good, you're here," Marq said. "We're just waiting for —"

The door slid open and Len, the *Reckoning's* chief science officer, hurried in. He was followed closely by Vay, their cultural programmer—scratch that, cultural *liaison*. All the cultural programmers had been reclassified after the High Council was destroyed, in an attempt to reflect how the Coalition of Planets had changed.

Len's brown hair was parted neatly on one side and slicked down with something and his blue eyes were unfocused, as usual. Vay's bright blue eyes were a little red around the edges, and her blonde hair brushed the collar of her uniform—a bit longer than regulation.

Nika's stomach sank. All of the command officers were here, plus two support personnel.

This is not going to be a quick mission.

Marq sat at the head of the table. Eric, Sorca, and Len sat on the far side, on Marq's left. Nika joined Vay in the seats on Marq's right, sitting across from the others.

"General Serath has pulled the *Reckoning* away from the Sol system and the Coalition colonies we're building there," Marq said. "I don't need to tell you how urgent that means this mission is."

He waited a moment for them to process that thought before saying, "We have been tasked with securing an audience with the Cygnians."

Nika actually laughed. She couldn't help herself. "The Cygnians?"

"That's really funny." Len laughed as well, but trailed off when no one else joined them. He craned his neck to look toward Marq. "Oh, you're serious. Is that why you had Vay and I prepare this report on Cygnus X-3?"

Marq nodded. "Proceed."

Len glanced around the table, holding Nika's gaze for a moment. She saw her own confusion and shock reflected in his face.

He cleared his throat and tapped on his bracer's control panel. A three-dimensional image of Cygnus-1 sprang up from the center of the table. It was so realistic, Nika felt like she could reach out and touch the crystalline surface of the planet.

"This is the Cygnian homeworld," Len said.

The planet was beautiful. It shimmered, light and rainbows skittering across its surface as it slowly rotated.

"Cygnus-1 is the only habitable planet orbiting the binary system of Cygnus X-3," Len said. "Their sun doesn't give off visible light, but it does emit a great deal of different forms of radiation."

"The intense radiation, plus the intense gravity fluctuations from the nearby black hole, have insulated the Cygnians from Coalition influence," Vay said.

Nika nodded. "Our shielding only allows us to travel the very outskirts of their system safely. I would love to see how their ships handle those challenges."

"I would love to see how the *Cygnians* survive it," Vay said.

Len tapped his bracer a few more times, and part of the surface of the planet disappeared, revealing the sub-surface beneath.

"The planet is protected by a layer of crystal that completely covers the atmosphere," he said. "We don't know exactly how, but the crystal layer both shields the planet from lethal levels of radiation and also creates the light and heat needed for life to survive."

"Wow," Nika said.

"We believe that's also why Cygnians possess skin that's impervious to most forms of energy weapons and many physical assaults," Vay said. "They had to evolve to handle what radiation made it through the crystal barrier."

"And don't forget the higher gravity levels." Len shook his head. "Cygnians are incredibly strong."

"If only our genetic engineers had been able to retain more of those traits when combining my Sadirian and Cygnian DNA." Sorca's smirk turned into a feral grin. "I would be even more effective in combat."

Eric lifted her hand to his lips and kissed it. "You're perfect just the way you are."

Sorca's eyes softened. "Such a sweet husband."

"If we could remain on topic," Marq said.

"We are focused, as always." Sorca leaned forward. "If

my increased strength and resilience is to be used as a measure, do not forget that I am more Sadirian than Cygnian. Their prowess will exceed my own."

"We aren't here to fight," Marq said. "Quite the opposite, in fact."

Vay turned to Marq, a deep crease between her eyebrows. "Sir, if you're hoping for an alliance, I don't believe that's possible. Historically, the Cygnians have always been strictly neutral. They're deeply loyal, but only to their own kind. We still don't know exactly how the High Council was able to secure the DNA that was used in Sorca's engineering."

"We may not know *why* the Cygnians gave us a DNA sample, but we do know the terms that were attached to it," Marq said. "Terms that the High Council violated."

"What?" Nika gasped.

"The High Council was only to have one Sadirian-Cygnian hybrid active at any time," Marq said. "To get around this limitation, they kept multiple clone copies of Sorca's body in a space station. Periodically, she would report to mental programming sites and have her most recent memories copied."

That was the exact protocol the High Council used for the ships in the Coalition's fleet. Downloads at space stations scheduled at regular intervals, along with repairs and systems checks.

"Why would they do that?" Nika said.

Marq clasped his hands together in front of him on the table. "We know that the High Council was performing experiments in reprogramming Sadirians, downloading information and even altering people's memories to serve their purposes."

Nika did not like where this was going.

"I am the greatest warrior in the fleet," Sorca said. "Before serving on the *Arbiter* under General Serath, I was sent on many missions. On those rare occasions when I failed, the High Council would activate another clone and download my most recent memories into a new body."

"Are you kidding me?" Nika nearly yelled.

Sorca just shrugged. "I do not remember my deaths. I was only made aware they had happened after they occurred."

Nika's jaw dropped open. She stammered a few incoherent sounds before saying, "They treated you like a machine."

"It is done," Sorca said. "This is my last body—my last life. And I gladly spend it with all of you."

Nika wanted to hit something. Preferably with an Earth-style wrench.

And if she was this mad on behalf of her friend, how the hell would the Cygnians—a warrior race who prized loyalty to their kind—react?

"Damage control," Nika said. "We need to do damage control."

Marq nodded. "We seek to prevent the Cygnians from entering the war on the side of the Tau Centauran Assembly."

Holy…

"Combining the advanced technologies of the Tau Centauran Assembly with the combat strength of the Cygnians would be devastating to our efforts in protecting our colonies," Nika said. "Even the Sol system might not be safe."

Marq shook his head. "The Vegans have assured us that they will take care of Sol's defense, and no sentients we have encountered can match their level of advancement. Earth is their homeworld now, and they will protect it."

"Well, this is worth missing Christmas for," Vay said. When everyone turned to her she gave a weak smile and shrugged. "It's an Earth holiday—and the reason Henry and I met. We were looking forward to spending it as a family."

The idea of Vay and her Earthling husband sitting around a tree with the enormous, white-furred Lyrians that had "adopted" him, almost made Nika laugh. The hugs would be epic, since Craig and Barbara each had four arms. And they had a new nestling due any time now.

It was such a…wholesome image. And Vay was missing out on that.

Nika suddenly understood Buddy's reaction to realizing he would miss his own family's celebration. She reached out and squeezed Vay's hand.

"I'm sorry you can't be with your family," Nika said.

Vay smiled at her. "They'll understand. And since I'm here, I took the opportunity to decorate the main crew lounge with a variety of the holidays celebrated around this time on Earth. After all, the *Reckoning* is just another sort of family."

Nika returned Vay's smile and nodded.

"Eric and I helped with the decorating." Sorca grinned broadly. "It is spectacular."

Nika didn't doubt it. She released Vay's hand and turned toward Marq.

"What do you need from me?" Nika said. "Your engineering crew should be up to any challenges you face out here."

"Actually, the *Reckoning* has been having an increasing number of malfunctions," Marq said. "Our engineers haven't been able to determine their cause. I need you to figure it out."

Nika nodded. If the ship's engineers were having trouble tracking it down, she had her work cut out for her.

"I'll get right on it," she said.

Marq stood. "We all have much to do. Vay and Len, work with Eric and Sorca to give me everything you can about Cygnian cultural protocols. I know we don't have much information, but remember, we're here to make things better, not worse. And Nika."

"Sir," she said.

"Fix my ship. Dismissed."

Nika nodded, then pushed herself back from the table. She rushed out into the hallway, tapping on her bracer to download the most recent readouts of the *Reckoning's* diagnostics and issue reports.

"Damn, that *is* a lot." She was surprised the *Reckoning's* engineers hadn't contacted her for help sooner.

Her bracer beeped as a new anomaly came up on the diagnostic check that had just finished. It wasn't too far out of the way to engineering. She turned down a hallway that was only used for maintenance and stopped in front of the mechanical cabinet with the issue.

"Let's see what you have for me," she said, opening the hatch.

A light flashed around the edges of the door and something hissed inside. It must be worse than she thought.

She froze as the door fully opened, her brain taking a moment to process what she was seeing.

A small reptilian humanoid was curled up in the cabinet, her scales dulled to an olive green instead of the usual emerald for her kind. The silver bands of her exosuit were as shiny as always.

A Vegan?

The bright blue that ran alongside of her darker stripes let Nika know who she was looking at.

"Cyan?" Nika said.

"Nika?"

There was a long pause while Nika ran through every scenario she could think of to explain why a Vegan—any Vegan—would be curled up in her mechanical cabinet. None of them made sense, so she just asked, "What are you doing here?"

"I am… Resting. Yes, resting."

"In a mechanical cabinet."

"It is quite a cozy fit for my frame," Cyan said. "And it is dim. Vegan eyes are more sensitive to light, you know."

"I didn't know that. But why wouldn't you just turn down the lights in your quarters if you were tired? Sleep in your own bed?"

"Yes." Cyan looked away. "That would make more sense, wouldn't it. Except I have not been assigned quarters."

And that makes no sense at all.

"What's going on?" Nika asked.

Cyan shifted a bit, then said, "I have been assigned by my people to learn as much as I can about Earth's life forms."

"Okay…"

"I am here to study Meredith's offspring."

Nika let out a huge breath, her shoulders relaxing. "You snuck on board so you could hang out with a bunch of kittens?"

Cyan sniffed a bit indignantly. "I am *studying* them."

"I get that they're super-cute, but… Does Marq even

know you're here?"

"No, and you must not tell him." Before Nika could protest, Cyan went on. "My research will be unduly influenced if the kittens or their humans know they are being observed."

"I didn't think Earth cats were that smart."

"They are not." Cyan leaned forward so quickly, she almost fell out of her hiding spot. She caught herself with her spindly green fingers, then pushed herself deeper into the cabinet. "I am a xenobiologist. I know what I am talking about."

"Well, I'm an engineer, and you're throwing off the *Reckoning's* self-diagnostics system." Nika gestured toward the cabling that Cyan was nestled against.

"I am truly sorry. I will be more cautious."

"Marq should know you're on board."

"Please…" Cyan begged. "We are trusted friends, are we not?"

Nika didn't know what to do. Even without a direct alliance, the Vegans were their most formidable defense. If she pissed off Cyan, what kind of ramifications might that have for the relations between the Coalition and her people?

Nika would have to think about what to do. *After* she fixed all the issues cropping up on the *Reckoning*.

"Just…keep the kittens away from my systems," Nika said.

"That is the idea," Cyan murmured, looking deeper into the mechanical cabinet.

"What?"

"Nothing." Cyan smiled and shifted closer to the door. "I will just get out of your way."

Cyan vanished right before Nika's eyes. Her exosuit's cloak was so complete, Nika didn't even see a ripple where the Vegan sat. She did hear a soft "thump" when Cyan hit the ground beside her.

"Thank you again," Cyan said.

"I…" Nika shook her head. "Sure."

She turned back to the cabinet, scanning for the issue that had caused the malfunction report in the first place. The insulation for some of the cabling had been torn away unevenly.

Nika leaned in closer, shining a light on the spot with her bracer. There was tons of tiny scoring all over the wiring—almost like scratch marks.

"What the hell?"

This mission was getting weirder and weirder. Nika needed to stay focused so she could get back to Buddy as quickly as she could.

As she started working on repairing the wiring, she remembered Marq's bondmate, Caitlin, warning them that cats had a knack for getting into places where they didn't belong. But these were just kittens. How would they be able to reach the systems that had been affected?

Nika was being ridiculous. Those marks could have been made by…electrical overloads. An engineer who was being careless with their tools.

Except, it really looked like deliberate tampering.

"Please, don't tell me we have a saboteur on board." With everything else going on, it was the last thing they needed.

Chapter Seven

"She got you good that time." Buddy laughed as he watched Patches and Pickles tussle on the floor. "You be careful with my dog."

Patches had the upper hand. Pickles was on his back, mouth wide and tongue hanging out as he clearly was having the time of his life. Patches arched up, ears flat against her head, then lunged, grabbing the dog around the neck.

Pickles managed to twist around and wriggle out of the kitten's grasp, running under the cot where Buddy was sitting. He waited for Patches to run after, and grabbed her before she could follow.

"I think that means he needs a time out," Buddy said. He scratched Patches behind her ears, smiling as she started to purr.

Patches stood up on his lap, her head barely reaching Buddy's chin. She butted her head against him, purring even louder.

"You are a sweetie, you know that?"

The door opened and the kitten scurried behind him.

Buddy's heart picked up as he looked over, expecting Nika. But no one was there. Again.

The door closed.

"What the heck is with that thing?" He looked down at Patches and saw her pressed close to his side, eyes wide and pupils swallowing up the gold of her irises as she stared at the door.

"Space cats do that, too, huh?" He started petting her head. "Do you see a ghost? Is that it?"

Patches started making little clicking noises. His mom's tabbies made a similar sound while stalking squirrels through the sliding glass door to the back yard.

"I'll take care of it for you," he said. He bent down and pulled out the picnic basket. "I like to watch documentaries about ghosts, and apparently, they don't like salt."

He opened the container that held the salt and pepper. As he reached for the salt, Patches let out a loud meow, startling him.

"Geeze, Patches. Don't scare me."

He sprinkled some salt in his palm without looking, then threw it in an arc across the small room. The sharp scent of pepper hit him, letting him know his mistake. He put his finger under his nose to keep from sneezing.

"Aw, crap," he said.

"Ah-choo!"

"Gesundheit." He glanced around the empty room. "Wait a minute."

The sneezing went on, coming from a few feet in front of the door. From the *absolutely nothing* right in front of the door.

"Holy crap, it *is* a ghost!" He grabbed Patches and pulled his feet from the floor. "Pickles, get up here!"

He heard whining from under the cot. Pickles seemed to like his hiding spot just fine.

The air shimmered after a particularly strong sneeze, revealing a three-foot tall lizard. A lizard standing up on its back legs and wearing shiny metal bands around its body.

"What the…"

The lizard blinked its huge gold eyes and rubbed its blunt nose. It looked a lot like his Uncle Teddy's iguanas.

"Cease your attack," it said, holding its hands up in front of itself.

"Attack? Wait, you mean the pepper? That was an accident."

The poor thing's eyes were watering like crazy. It let out another huge sneeze.

"Aw, man," Buddy said. "I'm sorry. I didn't mean to… Do you need some water or something to rinse your eyes out?"

"I think the worst of it has passed." The lizard…person shook its head vigorously and blinked again.

Wait… Lizard person…

"Hey, you're one of those lizard men, aren't you?" he said.

"Excuse me, I am a lizard *woman*."

"Oh, sorry. I didn't mean any offense." He tried to remember what Nika had called them. Something that made him think of food…

Vegans, that was it. But pronounced funny.

"Vegans," he said. "You're a Vegan."

"What? Me? No." The lizard lady shook her head, backing into the door. She spun around, ducking low, as if she expected the door to attack her.

"Nobody's going to hurt you," Buddy said. "I mean, besides that thing with the pepper. And, again, I'm sorry. I didn't see you there."

"Of course you didn't," she said. "I was cloaked."

"Cloaked. You mean invisible?"

"Close enough." She shook her head and spoke in a low voice, as if talking to herself. "There is nothing else for it." She approached him and extended her hand. "I am Cyan."

Buddy reached out and gently clasped her tiny fingers. "I'm Buddy."

He suddenly remembered that he was supposed to be hiding. But what was he supposed to do? There was no place to hide in here.

"Wait, Buddy of the sandwich shop?" Cyan said.

He let out a huge laugh. "Am I some kind of celebrity up here?"

"Your sandwiches are in high demand."

"I should open up a shop on board."

Cyan's eyes widened, her pupils narrowing to tiny slits. "That would be most wonderful! You could also build one on the new space station.

"Space station?"

"Yes, we are building a station called *Outreach* on the far side of Earth's moon. We will use the station as a meeting ground for many sentients—to establish a dialogue and further peace in the galaxy."

"*Earth's* moon?"

Cyan went on as if she hadn't heard him. "Sharing a delicious meal would be an excellent way to bridge the gap between different sentients."

She was talking about spreading peace in the galaxy... and she wanted to serve people Buddy's sandwiches?

"You should speak with Marq," Cyan said. "He is this ship's commander and is overseeing the work being done in the Sol system."

"That's all really nice of you to say, but I'm not even supposed to be here. I'd kind of appreciate it if you didn't tell anyone about me."

Cyan's eyes widened again and she shifted closer. "I am also not supposed to be here."

"I don't suppose you accidentally snuck on board to surprise someone with a Winter Solstice dinner?"

She cocked her head to the side in what was apparently a universally reptilian manner. "No..."

"Of course not." Buddy leaned back. "You guys

probably don't even have Winter Solstice. Or any of the winter holidays. No seasons on space ships to celebrate."

"Actually, we are trying to learn about Earth holidays." Cyan sat on the cot next to him, her legs dangling over the edge as she leaned forward to look at him. "Vay—she's a cultural liaison for the Sadirians—has decorated the main crew lounge with trappings from several holidays celebrated around this time of your planetary cycle."

"Really? That's great, I guess."

They sat in silence for a few moments, then Buddy said, "I was trying to impress Nika. To make her part of..." He shook his head. "I really messed things up with her."

"You love each other?" Cyan said.

"Whoa, what?" he stammered. "I don't... I mean..."

Cyan let out a little hissing breath that sounded a lot like laughter. "It would appear you are as bad at deception as I am."

Buddy gently rapped his head against the wall. He took in a deep breath, then blew it out forcefully.

"I don't know if she feels the same, but yeah, I love her," he said. "I was going to find the right time to tell her tonight during dinner. Then invite her to spend Christmas with my family."

"That sounds lovely," Cyan said.

"I never knew lizards could be so romantic."

She made a series of clicks and narrowed her eyes.

"Sorry, I'm not used to interacting with...space...

people," Buddy said. "I'd mind my manners, but I don't really know what they are."

"I shall bear with you."

He chuckled. "Thanks."

After another pause, Cyan said, "Nika also knows that I am here. She has promised to keep my secret."

"Well, I won't tell if you won't," Buddy said.

Cyan nodded. "An equitable exchange."

"If they find me, are they really going to give me a mind-wipe?"

His throat felt tight and his eyes burned at the thought of forgetting Nika. He really had messed everything up.

Cyan's eyes narrowed further. She let out a hiss-pop sound, her scales turning almost a livid green as she leapt to her feet, her tail thrashing behind her and spines running down the length of her body standing straight on end.

"You are an Earthling on a Coalition vessel," she said. "And I am a Vegan, sworn to protect Earthlings. If you wish to retain your memories, I will ensure it is so."

Damn...

In that moment, the three-foot-and-change tall lizard was one of the scariest things he'd ever seen in his life.

"I'm glad you're on our side," he said. "But if you stand up for me, they'll find out you're here."

"I will not sacrifice my principles merely to avoid an awkward situation."

"So, you won't get in trouble for being here?"

"For being here? No." She stepped back, clasping her hands together. Her scales returned to their normal emerald with blue and black stripes.

"Why *are* you here? If I can ask."

"I am a xenobiologist," Cyan said. "I study alien life forms."

Buddy imagined Cyan in a lab wearing a teeny white coat and staring at a hamster, scribbling notes on a clipboard. Damn, that would be cute.

"Okay," he said. "So, you're studying Earthlings or something?"

"My specialty is non-sentient animals," she said.

"Like cats and dogs."

Cyan nodded toward Patches. "I am particularly interested in cats. I have been studying them at great length and have befriended many. They have a fascinating perspective on existence."

"Wait, you can talk to them? Earth cats?"

"I can."

"You hear that?" He lifted the kitten to his cheek and kissed the top of her head. "She shouldn't have any kind of problem talking to *you*."

"Why…" Cyan clasped her hands in front of her. "Why do you say that?"

Buddy shrugged. "Because even I can understand Patches."

"You know her name?" Cyan's eyes widened.

"Yeah, she let me know. We're figuring out our own way to communicate," he said. "She may look like an Earth cat, but I've never met one as smart as her."

"She is…" Cyan swallowed hard, the tendons of her neck standing out for a moment, "quite intelligent. As are her brother and sister."

"There's a whole litter of them?" He turned to Patches and scratched her cheek. "I'd love to meet your family. Are they as smart as you? A whole family of super-smart space cats."

Cyan took a few steps closer. "They are not a space cats. They are *Earth* cats. They were just born on board the *Reckoning*."

"Okay…" Buddy wasn't sure why Cyan was being so emphatic about it.

"Just extremely smart Earth cats," Cyan said, staring at Patches. "That I am not sure what to do with."

"You treat them the same as any kids." He kissed the top of Patches's head again. "Give them lots of love and do your best to raise them right."

Cyan nodded. "Yes. I shall do my best. And I hope… I hope I can request your assistance from time to time. Your perspective seems quite pragmatic in such matters."

"I helped my parents raise four sisters," he said. "I should hope I learned a thing or two."

Patches started squirming against him. She leapt away as soon as he released her. The moment her paws hit the floor, Pickles came charging out from under the cot.

"Play nice," Buddy said.

"What is that?" Cyan yelled.

She jumped up onto the cot. The silver bands that wrapped around her arms, legs, and torso suddenly expanded to cover her body in shining armor. All he could see was her eyes.

Buddy jumped up, too, standing between Cyan and Pickles.

"Relax," he yelled. "That's just my dog, Pickles."

"A dog?" Cyan stared at the animals wrestling on the floor.

Thankfully, Patches once again had the advantage. Pickles was on his back with his paws waving in the air. The armor covering Cyan slid back in place as the small bands around her body. He had no idea how they'd done that.

"How exciting!" Cyan exclaimed.

"So, that's the Vegan technology I've heard so much about," he said, sitting cautiously beside her once more. "The tech that's going to protect Earth from the war."

Cyan cocked her head to the side again, but she kept staring Pickles as she spoke. "Nika has told you much."

Buddy blew out a breath. "Not nearly enough."

"This creature is fascinating," Cyan spoke as if she was mostly ignoring him, her attention fixed on his dog. "My exosuit tells me that over half of its volume is actually fur."

"Exosuit?"

"The bands of metal." She lifted her arm and gestured to the silver on her body.

He let out a nervous chuckle. "And here I thought you were just dressed up for the holidays."

That caught her attention enough for her to look at him. "My exosuit seems to be appropriate attire for your festivities?"

"Well, yeah. My family lives in Florida now, but we started out up North. We still like shiny things during the dark half of the year. It keeps our spirits up when the sun is down, so to speak. Come to think of it, those silver catsuits Nika and the others wear kind of fit the mood, too."

"Vay often wears colorful sweaters and has said it is in honor of Christmas—though she wears them almost year-round."

"An alien celebrating Christmas." He smiled. "I'd like to meet her. When it won't get Nika in trouble, of course."

"Of course. I am certain Vay would like that very much." Cyan looked up at the door. "But for now, I must take my leave. Nika is approaching."

"Nika?"

Buddy's mouth went dry. His heart was suddenly a drum in his chest.

"If she sees Patches in here, she'll wonder how she got in," Buddy said.

"I will take Patches with me."

Cyan hurried forward and plucked the kitten off of Pickles. She disappeared a moment later. The kitten didn't.

"Cyan…"

"Vapor pits! Pardon my language. I have been spending too much time with Zemanni. My cloak does not cover what I carry."

The kitten was floating through the room, completely visible. She suddenly flew up toward the ceiling and stayed there, a lot like the Antarean had in the hangar bay.

"Nika will see," Cyan said. "Can you distract her?"

"Yeah. Yeah, I'll do my best." Buddy stood and stared at the door.

How the hell was he supposed to distract Nika from a kitten floating near her ceiling? The room was so small, Buddy could almost touch the ceiling just be stretching.

The door slid open and Nika hurried in, a large cylinder hovering behind her. With everything he'd seen, it didn't even faze him.

Her brow creased when she saw Buddy. "Are you okay?" she asked.

Patches floated toward the door as Cyan made her way to the exit. Nika started to turn, following Buddy's gaze. She was going to see Cyan.

Buddy grabbed Nika's arms.

Aw, hell…

He pulled her close and kissed her.

Chapter Eight

Buddy's hands gripped her arms tight, keeping Nika pressed against his chest. His mouth demanded her full attention, stealing her breath away. She gasped, and his tongue slid between her lips.

Heat flooded through her. Her legs weakened, but he held her up, crushing her to him as they melted together.

She had kissed people before, but never like this.

Slowly, his kiss grew more gentle, letting her feel his softness, his warmth. His tongue explored more than conquered.

The molten sensation flowing along her nerves spread further, lighting up her skin and pooling between her legs. She wrapped her arms around his waist, pulling him closer. She wanted more.

The anti-grav pod she'd linked up to her bracer flew across the room, following the movement of her arm. It hit the wall with a loud crash. Buddy broke off the kiss at the sound, urging her behind him as he spun around to see what it was.

"Relax," Nika said. She tapped the commands on her

bracer that deactivated the pod, letting it sink slowly to the floor.

Buddy turned back to her and ran one hand through his hair. He stammered a few incomprehensible things before saying, "Sorry. I should have asked first. I just…"

"You just what?" Nika swallowed hard, struggling to catch her breath.

Buddy smiled at her gently. He shook his head and shrugged.

"I'm just crazy about you," he said.

"Crazy?"

"It's an expression. An Earth expression. What I'm trying to say is… I love you."

"Oh." She smiled back and let out a small laugh as the full meaning of his words hit home. Buddy loved her.

"I love you, too," she said.

"You do?"

Her smile broadened and she nodded. "Yeah."

"That's… That's incredible."

He laughed, then picked her up and started spinning her around in the small space. She locked her legs onto his waist and clung to him, joining in his laughter.

With everything going on, she couldn't believe she could feel so light. And yet here she was, happier than she had ever been in her life. She held onto the feeling as tightly as she held to Buddy.

Pickles ran over to them and started jumping up and

barking. Buddy leaned over to shush him.

"Come on, Pickles," he said. "Knock it off."

"It's okay. My quarters are sound-proofed, remember?"

"Yeah, but he's killing the mood. I wish you had another room in here."

"The bathroom's right through that door." She really should have shown him where that was before she left.

"Where?" Buddy turned them around so he was facing the direction she'd nodded.

She laughed again and pointed. "I forget you're used to more obvious doors."

He didn't set her down, but walked them over to the bulkhead. Nika reached out and ran her fingertip over the etching on the wall that opened the bathroom door.

"That's the bathroom?" Buddy said.

"Yes."

With nothing activated, all the devices were stored within the walls. No wonder he seemed confused. They were staring into what looked like a small, completely empty closet.

"You're going to have to explain that to me later," Buddy said.

"Okay."

He put his hands on her waist and gently set her on her feet, then took off his jacket.

"Is there anything that would be dangerous for Pickles in there?" he asked.

"No."

"Awesome." He tossed his jacket into a corner of the room, then nodded toward Pickles. "Hey, Pickles. Go check out the bathroom. And stay there."

The dog trotted into the room, sniffing the edges of the walls. He curled up on Buddy's jacket and closed his eyes.

"That's one less thing to distract us," Buddy said.

"Distract us from what?"

"From this." He pulled her close and kissed her again.

All the passion of that first kiss was back, only this time, deepened now that she knew how he felt about her. They were in love. They would figure out a way to make this work.

She wrapped her arms around his neck, lifting herself up so she could kiss him more deeply. Buddy let out a groan. His hands slid down to her ass and squeezed.

He kissed his way to her ear and murmured, "I've dreamt about this every night since you walked into my place."

"Me, too."

"Seriously?" He leaned back, smiling. "Then we have a lot of time to make up for." He grabbed the hem of his shirt and pulled it over his head, then tossed it away.

Nika was stunned at the complexity of the markings on his skin. She caught her lower lip between her teeth and reached out, trailing her fingertips over the slightly raised surface of the designs. "I have wanted to touch these forever."

"Have at it."

Buddy stood still, smiling as she circled him. The markings—tattoos—went up over his shoulders, down his arms and back. Some were swirling patterns, some images of things she recognized or didn't. A few words were sprinkled through.

Every tattoo had to have a story behind it. She couldn't wait to learn each one.

The muscle beneath them was also calling her attention, and making more of that core-reactor heat spread through her body. His broad back tapered down to a narrow waist. His jeans stretched across the muscles of his thighs and showcased his magnificent ass. His forearms were corded, his biceps huge.

She stopped in front of him again, tracing the lines of his abdomen down to the waistband of his jeans. An equally impressive bulge strained against his zipper.

"Nika, I'm barely holding it together, here," he said.

"I don't want you to hold it together. I want... I want you."

"I'm already yours."

He grabbed the back of her neck and pulled her in for a crushing kiss. His tongue slid into her mouth, claiming everything.

She reached between them and unfastened his pants, giving her room to reach in and stroke his shaft. As she wrapped her fingers around his thickness, he let out a groan that she could feel vibrate through his chest. He broke off the kiss, lowering his head to her shoulder as she continued to squeeze and stroke him.

"There are things my friends have told me about Earth sex," she said.

"You seem to know what you're doing." His fingers curled against her back.

She started to lower herself to her knees, wanting to experiment, to experience everything with him. Buddy gripped her arms and kept her upright.

"If you do that, I won't last two seconds," Buddy said. He started kissing her neck, nipping and sucking on her skin. "I want to be inside you. It's killing me how much I want it."

Her skin rose in gooseflesh both from his words and his warm breath against her ear. They would have time to explore each other later—she hoped.

She stepped away from him, nodding.

"Then you'd better strip," she said.

Buddy laughed, backing up to the cot and sitting down. He started unlacing his shoes as she unsealed the collar of her uniform.

"Hang on a minute." He kicked off his shoes. "I want to watch you."

Nika froze, unsure how to react. She'd had sex with other Sadirians before, but only using *Coupling*—the drug the Coalition provided to citizens to…basically handle the whole thing for them. No one had ever wanted to watch her undress.

Buddy pulled off his socks and threw them aside, then stood. He hooked his thumbs in the waistband of his jeans. Slowly, his gaze locked on her face, he tugged them down his legs.

The soft sounds of the fabric, the slow reveal of more skin… She started to understand why he wanted to watch her.

When his jeans hit the floor, he stepped out of them. His boxer-briefs couldn't hide his arousal. Especially since they hit the floor next.

"I want you to see what you do to me," Buddy said.

Nika swallowed hard, eyes locked on his dick as it jutted toward her. She could already imagine what it would feel like, their bodies connected in the most intimate way.

She forced her gaze back to his face. Lifting her hands to her collar, she pulled the shiny fabric open.

Her breath caught in her throat as she watched how his expression changed. As she unsealed more of her uniform, his smile faded. A muscle in his jaw stood out enough that she could see it through the stubble that was quickly turning into a beard.

She unfastened her belt and let her uniform slide down her arms, following it to the floor so she could unseal her boots. When she stepped out of them—only wearing her undergarments—she became hyper-aware of the cool air in her quarters touching her skin. She wanted it to be Buddy's hands instead.

She wasn't the only one. Buddy closed the distance between them.

"I changed my mind." He kissed her, his hands clasping her waist. The roughness of his skin sent gooseflesh over her body in waves.

He slid his palms up her sides, fingers roving under the edge of her sports bra. He pulled the fabric up and over her head, then let it drop to the ground.

His chest against hers, nothing between them but heat and friction… Tingling arcs snapped out from her core like an engine about to overload. He palmed a breast, squeezing it and rubbing his thumb across her nipple till it tightened and ached. He dropped his head to her chest, soothing her breast with his mouth even as he tormented the other with his touch.

"Buddy…"

He slid her briefs down, and pulled in a hissing breath through his teeth as he looked at her. "God, you're beautiful. Every part of you."

Plenty of crewmates had seen her naked. With limited space, it was hard to have privacy. But no one, not even her past lovers, had ever looked at her like this.

"I think I'm going to go crazy if I don't fuck you right now," he said.

"That…sounds good to me. I mean, the second part. Not the going crazy."

He let out a chuckle. "Only you could make me laugh in the middle of this and have that make it even better." He stood before her, hands on either side of her neck as he ran his thumbs along her jaw. "I want to share everything with you."

"I want that, too."

But how could she? She had obligations. Her people were counting on her.

"None of that," he said. "I get it now. What you're thinking when you make that face. What you're feeling."

"And what am I feeling?"

"A burden."

Her stomach twisted as the truth of it hit her like a blow to the chest.

"A burden no one should have to carry alone," he said.

Her eyes filled with tears. Blast it, she never cried. Ever. She wouldn't now. Not during this.

Buddy leaned in and kissed her, once again rescuing her from herself. She let her thoughts, her worries, her fears, her *obligations* all go and just lost herself in his touch.

Chapter Nine

This was heaven. Nika in his arms, nothing between them.

She was so beautiful. And, damn, she was strong. So much stronger than he'd even realized.

The weight she was carrying would have crushed anyone else he knew. But he was going to help her carry it now. No one could stop him.

He ran his fingers down her stomach and through her curls, not stopping as he spread her slit. She gasped against his mouth and he held her tighter.

This was going to be amazing for her. As amazing for her as it would be for him. He just had to make sure she was ready first.

He slid two fingers in, his thumb circling her clit. Her gasp turned into a moan.

He moved inside her, his dick pulsing, aching to take over.

Just a little more.

Flexing his fingers, he massaged her core, stretching her bit by bit.

"Buddy…"

"I love it when you say my name." He buried his face in the nape of her neck, breathing in her scent.

"I want you," she said. "Please."

How could he resist that?

He lifted her from the ground, urging her to wrap her legs around his waist as he reclaimed her mouth. They staggered to a wall. The cot didn't look strong enough for what he had in mind and he didn't know if the two of them could fit in the techno-bed.

As soon as her back hit the wall, he reached between them and lined up his dick.

God, she was so hot and wet. He kissed her harder, trying to keep himself from just ramming into her.

Slowly, he pushed himself in, savoring every sensation. Her sheath wrapped around him, holding him tight.

Fire flooded his veins and his heartbeat pounded in his ears as his entire reality shrank down to just this—the feel of her, the connection he'd never felt with anyone else before.

His control snapped, and he thrust into her, deep, pinning her to the wall with his dick.

Nika's fingernails raked across his back, her hips shimmying against his. If she kept that up, he wouldn't last long enough. And he wanted to hold onto every moment of this.

He pulled out slowly, almost all the way, then thrust

back into her. Her heels dug into his ass, urging him on.

The next stroke was harder, faster, as he set a relentless pace that she matched with each movement of her body. Her core squeezed his shaft, her hips arced to meet every thrust.

The heat built inside him, pressure rising deep in his gut as all he could think about was where they were joined.

Nika cried out his name, clawing at his back as her core pulsed against him. That was all it took to send him over the edge.

His thrusts became frenzied as he rammed into her over and over again, pleasure exploding through his body in deafening waves. She clung to him, taking everything he had to give.

Finally spent, he held her against the wall, listening to the sound of their heavy breaths.

"Thank you," Nika said.

"Any time." Buddy chuckled and kissed the side of her neck. He leaned back so he could look her in the eyes. "Seriously, any time you want. That was amazing."

She smiled, her eyes heavy-lidded. "Yeah, it really was."

Something in the room beeped. Loudly.

"What the heck is that?" Buddy asked.

She covered his mouth with her hand. "Communications request. Shh."

He smirked and nodded.

She lowered her hand and said, "Open channel. Nika

here."

Buddy leaned in and kissed her neck, sucking hard on her skin. She gasped and he chuckled against her.

"Hi, Nika." A woman's voice spoke. "I just thought you'd want to know that we'll be dropping out of blue space in half an hour."

"Thanks, Vay." Nika swatted Buddy's shoulder and he stopped.

"How did the decorations work out for you?" Vay said.

"Decorations? Oh, right. I haven't gotten them up yet."

Buddy arced an eyebrow. She clamped a hand over his mouth again, but was smiling.

"Do you need help?" Vay asked. "I can stop by."

"No, no," Nika said. "You have your hands full researching the Cygnians. Everything's under control here. But I'll be sure to call if I need you."

"Okay." There was a wistful note to Vay's voice. Buddy wondered if the two women were friends.

"See you soon, then," Vay said.

"Right."

A quieter beep sounded. Maybe that meant the transmission had ended?

Nika let go of Buddy's mouth. Probably that meant the transmission had ended.

She also let go of her grip with her legs. Buddy held her as she slid back to the ground.

"Knees a little wobbly?" he asked.

"All of me's a little wobbly."

"So, what decorations was Vay talking about?"

Nika smirked, and led him by the hand to the cylinder that had floated into the room after her when she'd first arrived.

"You wanted to share your traditions with me," Nika said. She knelt down and opened the cylinder.

Inside, it was filled with tinsel, ornaments, Christmas lights, and even a tiny tree. Buddy dropped to his knees beside her.

"Oh, this is great! We can really..." he looked around her absolutely barren room, "spruce this place up."

"There are adhesives to attach things to the walls, and I figure we can put the tree on my regen bed."

"Is that the fancy techno-bed under the tarp?"

"'Techno-bed'?" She shook her head. "That's a nicer name for it."

"I wanted to ask, why do you sleep on a cot when you have that thing?"

"The regen beds are supposed to heal us overnight as we sleep."

"That doesn't sound like a bad thing," Buddy said.

"It isn't, but we also have programming pods. They're supposed to be used to download information that's useful in missions. We learned the languages of Earth and other useful data that way."

"Wait, *all* the languages of Earth?"

She shrugged, shifting to sit next to the container. "We never know where we'll be needed."

"That sounds amazing."

"Yeah, that part's pretty cool. But not too long ago, we found out that our government had integrated programming technology into some of our regen beds and was using it to change our memories and even our personalities, if it suited their purposes. Without telling us."

"Holy shit. Did someone stop them?"

"You could say that. The Tau Centauran Assembly… They destroyed our homeworld. Sadr-4. And all of our colonies in our home system."

Her planet had been nuked? Damn. Buddy figured things were bad, since she had to build new homes for her people. But this took it to a whole new level.

"I'm sorry," he said.

"Me, too. With the High Council gone—that was our ruling body—our new leader is the head of the fleet, General Serath. He goes by Adam Smith on Earth."

"That's a really fake-sounding name," Buddy said.

"He didn't think he'd be that involved with Earth, but then he married an Earthling."

Buddy smiled, despite the gravity of the conversation. "No kidding?"

"If the Tau Centauran Assembly would just listen to us, we could stop this war," Nika said. "The High Council started it, and they're gone."

"But this Assembly, they're not interested in stopping."

Nika nodded. "I just found out our mission, and it's really important. The Tau Centaurans are trying to bring the Cygnians into the war on their side. If that happens, I don't know what will become of us."

"Even with the Vegans helping out?"

"Yes."

"What about Earth? Are we still safe, now that you know what's going on?"

"I don't know. I hope so."

Buddy sat on the floor next to her. He glanced over at all the bright and colorful decorations, more scared than he'd ever been in his life. He ran his hand over his face, took a deep breath, then blew it out.

"It's going to be okay," he said.

"What?"

He forced a smile, willing himself to feel it. "It's going to be okay. You said you want to share my traditions. Well, this time of year is all about hope. It's about miracles and having faith that things will work out. That's why we light all these lights. To push back the darkness. To remind us there's still hope."

Nika pulled her lips between her teeth and pressed her mouth shut tight. Her eyes filled with tears again. His Nika. The strongest woman he knew.

"Hey, none of that." He clasped her face in his hands and leaned forward to kiss her. When he pulled back, he didn't have to fake his smile.

"It *is* going to be okay," he said.

"How can you be so sure?"

"Because look at all the miracles surrounding us right now. You and me, together. What are the odds we'd find each other across this whole universe?"

She smirked and cocked her head to the side. "I guess they're pretty slim."

"*You guess.*" He reached for her hand and used it to pull her into his lap. "It's a bonafide miracle that someone as smart and gorgeous as you could fall for a guy like me."

"What do you mean?"

"I make sandwiches. You make spaceships and…dome worlds."

"You forget, you're famous for your sandwiches out here."

"Yeah, I guess that's true."

She laughed, but then quieted. "I'm sorry you're going to miss Christmas with your family."

He shrugged. "I'm with them in my heart. And now, you're my family, too."

Chapter Ten

Nika's chest was so full, she didn't know how her ribs were keeping themselves together. She couldn't believe how relieved she felt that Buddy finally understood why she had to keep leaving him.

The warmth fled as she realized she would still have to keep leaving him. And some day, she might get an assignment that meant she couldn't go back.

"You know that I would stay with you on Earth if I could," she said.

"Of course. But I also know that your people need you."

"I don't know how much time we'll have together."

"Stop. You're making that face again." He gently cupped her cheek, then leaned in for a light kiss. "Nobody knows how much time they have. And I'm not the clingy type. I know how to keep myself busy while you're working. I have my own things."

It seemed too good to be true. But then, he had said this was a time for miracles.

He laughed and said, "Maybe you can add some sub shops to your designs. Since my sandwiches are so famous and all."

"That's not a bad idea."

"But I'm proud of my work," he said. "I'll have to do on-site inspections—which may just coincide with your assignments, wherever they are. I have to make sure everything's up to my standards."

"You sound like me."

"We take care of people. We build stuff for them. My stuff just gets eaten."

Nika laughed.

"And hey, you should put a sub shop on *Outreach*."

"*Outreach*?"

"Yeah, the space station behind the...moon..." He looked away as he finished. "That I'm not supposed to know about."

"How do you know about *Outreach*?"

He let out a huge sigh, then said, "Cyan told me."

"Cyan? Cyan was here?"

"She was just chasing after one of those space cats."

Nika shook her head, her thoughts spinning. "Start at the beginning."

"Okay, I was hanging out waiting for you, then the door opened a crack. Before I could try to hide, this little kitten came running in." He laughed, then said, "Scared the dickens out of her to see me, I think."

Nika arched a brow at him. He cleared his throat and went on.

"She and Pickles really hit it off," Buddy said. "They played for a while, then the door opened again. I didn't see anybody come in that time, but that's because it was Cyan. I kinda threw some pepper at her by accident and she decloaked when she had a sneezing fit."

"You threw pepper at a Vegan?" Nika yelled.

"I thought she was a ghost! And I thought it was salt."

"What does... How does..." Nika shook her head. Buddy's explanation wasn't helping her make sense of this.

"It was just a misunderstanding. But we sorted it out, and now we're friends." He chuckled, and said, "You don't have to worry about me getting a mind-wipe, either. She says while I'm here, I'm under her protection. I don't think Marq's going to dare cross her. She's super-cute, but she can be really scary."

"That's... I think I need to sit down."

Buddy wiggled his knees, bouncing her in his lap. "You are sitting."

"Then I think I need to lay down."

He looked over at the cot, then back at her, a broad smile on his face.

"Don't you tempt me," she said. "We're dropping out of blue space soon, which means we're almost to the rendezvous point. If we're going to decorate, we better get to it."

"We could skip decorating and..." He looked back at the cot.

"I told Vay I was decorating. If she stops by and sees that I didn't, she'll wonder why. Cyan's protection aside, I'd rather my crewmates not find out about you."

"Right. Cyan did ask me to keep it secret that she's on board. But she let me know that you already knew."

"Okay, then. Decorating."

They both rose to their feet.

"Maybe we should get dressed first." Buddy looked into the cylinder. "It'd be weird putting up Christmas stuff naked."

"It's your tradition. I fabricated a uniform for you." She pulled the silver garment from the container.

"I thought that was just more tinsel."

As she held it up for him, his smile faded. "No way. I'm not wearing that."

"Everyone on board wears the same uniform," she said. "It's not just to make you less conspicuous, but also for your safety. If there's a hull breach, this is the only thing that will keep you from suffocating."

He frowned, shifting his weight from one foot to the other.

"Buddy."

"I'm thinking."

She tossed the uniform to him and he caught it.

"Fine," he said. "But you need to design something to protect Pickles, too."

"That's a really good point. I'll get on it as soon as I

can."

She grabbed her own clothing and quickly dressed. Buddy had managed to mostly get his on, but his uniform wasn't sealed.

"How the heck does this thing work?" he said.

Nika laughed as she approached. "There are seals and release points."

She bent down and locked his boots, then ran her fingers up along the main seal over his abdomen. She locked his collar and checked that the helmet contained within had access to deploy in case of emergencies, then sealed his belt.

"I'm never getting out of this thing," he said.

"The release points are here, here, and here." She tapped the spots on his collar, belt, and boots as she spoke.

"I feel ridiculous."

"You look pretty hot, actually."

He snorted and looked away.

"I mean it," she said.

"I guess I should get used to it, if I'm going to open sandwich shops around the galaxy."

"Buddy…"

"Let a guy dream." He stepped closer, running his hands up and down her arms. "We'll figure that out later. Let's get to decorating."

"Where do we start?" she asked.

"Well…" He reached into the container and pulled out a

pair of furry red hats with white trim. After handing her one, he placed the other on his head. "It helps to look the part."

"O…kay." She put on the hat, watching as he picked up the tree and set it on the tarp covering her regen bed.

"We can do the tree first. Oh, but we need some music."

He ran to the bathroom and returned with his phone. After messing with it for a moment, light, festive music filled the room. For some reason, Nika couldn't keep herself from smiling as she heard it.

"It's not your heavy metal, but—"

"It's lovely," she said.

It didn't take long for them to turn her dull, small quarters into a bright, festive space. They stood in the center, turning in circles and looking at the lights and the glittering tinsel covering the walls.

"Wow," Nika said. "This looks like your house."

"I don't do things half-way." He put his hands on her hips and pulled her close. "Or didn't you notice?"

Nika laughed, wrapping her arms around his neck. "Oh, I noticed. I also noticed decorating my quarters didn't take as long as I expected."

"You have something in mind?"

"Well, Sorca did tell me once about something called a 'quickie'."

Buddy laughed. "I'll thank her if I ever get to meet her."

He leaned in for a kiss just as the door to her chamber

opened. Nika leapt away—as if distancing herself from him could keep him safe. But the door only opened a crack.

Patches came running in. She paused, ears perked when she saw Nika. The kitten rushed forward and started circling Nika's ankles and meowing.

"I missed you, too." Nika bent down to pick up the kitten. "But how in the name of the Solar Cross did you open my door?"

Patches was purring loudly, the sound vibrating through the kitten's small body.

"Wow, and I thought you liked *me*." Buddy reached over and scratched behind the kitten's ears. "Clearly, Nika is your favorite."

"Patches does seem to gravitate toward me."

"Pickles will be crushed."

The little dog trotted out from the bathroom, letting out a huge yawn. As soon as Patches saw him, she squirmed in Nika's arms until she knelt and let her down.

"Remember, be careful with my dog," Buddy said. "He's not as smart as you."

It was sort of strange that he was talking to Patches directly. Almost like how Marq spoke to his cats. But then, Marq was their owner.

"Pickles is pretty smart," Nika said.

Buddy laughed. "Not as smart as a space cat."

"Patches is a regular Earth cat."

"That's what Cyan said, but I'm not buying it. That

kitten is super-smart."

"Oh, come on."

Buddy gestured to the door. "If she's a regular cat, how does she keep getting into your quarters? Last I saw her, Cyan was carrying her out of here, which means she also got away from your Vegan friend, with all her advanced technology."

Nika stared at the pair of animals chasing each other around her quarters. How *had* Patches managed to open the door? Twice, even.

Nika thought back to the mechanical cabinet that she'd investigated when she first came aboard—and the dozen other areas that had the same kind of strange damage. Small scoring, as if they'd been picked at with a needle-like tool. Just enough damage to cause a problem, but not enough to harm the ship.

Could Patches have been trying to get my attention?

Nika knew she was the kitten's favorite. Marq had said so half a dozen times. But an animal responsible for sabotage? That was just insane.

Pickles gained the upper hand, pinning Patches to the ground. The kitten hissed, rolling over and managing to squirm out of Pickles's grasp. She bolted for the door, jumped up, batted at the access panel, then landed on the ground…just as the door opened.

"What the hell?" Nika said.

How had Patches figured out the control pattern to open

the door? It wasn't like it was a simple tap or swipe.

Patches ran out the door, Pickles on her heels.

"Pickles!" Buddy ran after his dog.

"Buddy, no!" Nika yelled, following them all.

She reached the hall just as Buddy disappeared around a corner.

Chapter Eleven

"Buddy!" Nika called out his name again.

Buddy couldn't stop, though. He was barely keeping up with Pickles as it was.

"I'm not leaving my dog," he yelled back.

"I can track him and we can find him later."

"But he might get hurt."

He heard Nika's exasperated groan, but dammit, this was his dog! He had to keep Pickles safe.

"Patches, stop," Buddy yelled. "You're going to get us all in trouble."

He skidded to a stop as Pickles ran out into a large open space. Buddy leapt back, throwing out a hand to stop Nika from turning the corner.

There were people out there. A tall blond man and a short brunette.

Buddy held a finger to his lips to let Nika know to be silent, then peered around the corner.

Patches ran straight to the man…and then straight *up* his body.

"Patches," the man said. "How in the name of the Solar

Cross do you keep escaping from our quarters?"

The kitten perched on the man's shoulder, and Buddy swore she was grinning at Pickles. The dog, for his part, was leaping into the air and barking frantically, trying to reach his playmate.

"What the heck?" the woman said, eyes wide as she stared at Pickles.

Nika tugged on Buddy's arm, pulling him back from the corner. She mouthed, "We have to go."

Buddy shook his head and whispered, "I'm not leaving my dog."

Nika stepped closer. "That is Marq and Caitlin—the commander of the *Reckoning* and his bondmate. We do not want Marq to find you here."

"But…"

Buddy looked back around the corner. Marq was holding Pickles now. The dog was squirming like crazy, so Marq held him against his chest, which, of course, gave Pickles a chance to start licking the guy.

"I don't understand what's happening." Marq held Pickles out to Caitlin. "You told me the kittens would undergo changes as they grew, but this…"

"That's a dog, honey." She took hold of the wriggly dog, hugging him close and getting the same treatment of kisses. She laughed, and said, "And a super-sweet one at that. Who's a good doggie? Yes you are. But where the heck did you come from?"

"What's a dog?" Marq said.

Who the hell doesn't know what a dog is? Oh right. Aliens.

"A dog is another Earth creature," Caitlin said. "The real question is, how did this little guy get on board the ship?"

Pickles started barking at Patches again. Marq looked back and forth between them, then asked, "Can dogs talk?"

Caitlin sighed. "No. Dogs can't talk. And neither can cats."

"So you say."

Patches took that moment to launch herself off of Marq's shoulder. Pickles lurched against Caitlin, and she barely had time to squat and let him escape from a safer height.

"Patches," Marq yelled, giving chase.

Trouble was, the cat was leading them straight toward Buddy and Nika.

"Shit," Buddy hissed.

Nika grabbed his arm and pulled him into a small room that she'd unlocked. It was barely big enough for the two of them. The door slid shut behind them, leaving them in darkness.

"Do you think they'll—" His thought was cut off as the door opened again.

They both looked down to see Patches sitting on the ground, staring up at them. Her tail flicked back and forth as Pickles tried to pounce on it.

"Traitor," Buddy said.

Marq and Caitlin ran up behind the animals. They both stared at Buddy and Nika, crammed into the closet.

"What's…going on here?" Caitlin asked, gesturing to the pair.

"We're just making out," Buddy said. "You know how it is."

Caitlin's eyebrows rose. "Wow, you're almost as bad of a liar as Cyan."

"The cute little—" His breath rushed out as Nika elbowed him in the stomach. "I mean, I don't know Cyan."

"Step forward," Marq said.

Damn, that guy had a commanding voice.

Buddy and Nika spilled out of the closet. He hadn't felt like this since High School, when his little sister, Becca, caught him under the bleachers with one of the school's cheerleaders.

"Explain," Marq said.

"Commander, this is…" Nika looked at Buddy, then back to Marq. "This is exactly what it looks like."

"Wait, what?" Buddy said.

"This is Buddy," Nika said, gesturing to him.

Caitlin's face lit up. "The sub shop guy?"

Buddy smiled. "That's me. And free sandwiches for life if you let me keep my memories."

"Nika." Marq said.

"Hey, listen, pal." Buddy stepped forward, getting in

Marq's face. "You have lots of people who are falling for Earthlings and even marrying them. Now that it's happened to Nika, you're going to try to stop her?"

To his credit, the other man didn't back down or puff up. He just stared at Buddy intently.

"I know how much you need her," Buddy said. "But I need her, too. And she needs me. Whether she knows it or not."

"Buddy…" Nika reached out and clasped his hand. He stepped back to stand beside her.

"I love you," he said, staring down at her. "And I'm going to fight like crazy to be with you." He turned back to Marq and said, "So bring it on."

Caitlin let out a laugh. "Wow, he sounds just like Sorca. Only… Earth-style. You know."

Buddy didn't know what that meant. But Caitlin was laughing, and she was Marq's girl, so hopefully it was a good sign.

Marq turned to Nika and said, "You fell in love with the sandwich maker?"

"Have you *tried* his sandwiches?" she asked.

Marq nodded his head, a grave expression on his face. "I have."

Buddy almost wanted to laugh. Marq's serious demeanor was adding a surreal quality to the whole thing.

"Why are you wearing those hats?" Marq asked.

"We were decorating Nika's quarters." Buddy shrugged.

He'd forgotten they were wearing them. "Getting into the spirit of the season. You know?"

"Not really," Marq said.

"Well, we can teach you."

Marq lifted his chin, his gaze going to Nika. "You've finished all the repairs to the *Reckoning.*"

Nika nodded. "Yes, sir."

"Have you discovered their source?" Marq asked.

"It looks like someone tampered with the cabling in several low-level systems," she said. "The insulation was stripped off and some of the wires were touching that shouldn't be."

He angled his head slightly. "A saboteur?"

"Yes, but..." Nika looked over at Buddy. He squeezed her hand, hoping to reassure her.

"But?" Marq prompted.

"I have a theory," she said. "But it's pretty out there."

He nodded. "Proceed."

"You remember how Patches always seemed to just show up wherever I was working on the *Reckoning*?" Nika said. "Before I was reassigned?"

"Yes, she has an amazing skill at getting where she isn't supposed to be," Marq said.

Caitlin leaned forward. "I did warn you about that."

"Well, I would talk to her while I worked," Nika said. "Explain what I was doing. And...the marks on the wires... They kind of look like claw marks."

Caitlin laughed long and hard. "That's…" She calmed herself when she realized she was the only one laughing.

"You think Patches did this?" Marq asked.

"Okay, stop," Caitlin said. "I am the veterinarian here, and I'm telling you for the last time, cats are just not that smart."

Patches let out a snort.

Caitlin stared down at her, eyes narrowing. She shook her head briskly. "There's no way an Earth cat could do that."

"Ah, but she's a *space* cat," Buddy said. "She was born on the ship, right?"

"Yeah…" Caitlin arched a brow at him.

"Couldn't there have been like cosmic radiation or something that mutated her DNA?" Buddy said.

Caitlin laughed again. "You've been reading too many comic books."

"Said the lady standing on a space ship wearing a silver catsuit." Buddy crossed his arms over his chest and leaned forward.

"Okay," she said. "Point taken."

"The ship filters out harmful radiation." Nika said.

"And yet…" Marq stared hard at Patches, then turned to Caitlin. "You will scan her for anomalies."

"Sweetie?" Caitlin cast a withering smile at him, one Buddy had seen too many times from his sisters.

By Buddy's calculations, Marq had about five seconds

to get his bacon out of the fire.

Marq straightened. "I mean, would you please scan her for anomalies? Len and his team will provide you with all the support you need."

Caitlin nodded. "That's better. And yes, I will work with Len to check all of your kittens' DNA against other cats'. I'll even check Meredith's as well. But we don't have a control group, so it'll have to wait till we're back on Earth."

"I appreciate your assistance," Marq said.

"So, she's not one of your crew?" Buddy asked.

"Caitlin is an Earthling," Marq said. "And she is my bondmate."

Buddy clapped his hands. "I knew it! Even *you* have an Earthling wife. Now you have to let Nika and I date."

"No one is trying to stop you," Marq said.

"Wait, what?" Nika said. "You're not going to give him a mind-wipe and tell me I need to focus?"

Marq hissed in a breath, his jaw tightening enough to make the tendons pop out. He looked down at the floor and slowly exhaled. It was the biggest reaction Buddy had seen from the guy, and kind of floored him after how even Marq had been before.

"That is the old way," Marq said. "And one I will *never* follow."

He looked back to Nika and straightened. "You are the best engineer in the fleet. You work tirelessly for our people

—for everyone who has been displaced in this war. If having Buddy as part of your life supports you in your efforts, I will not allow anyone to stand in the way of that. Do you understand?"

Nika pulled her lips between her teeth, pinching them tight. She nodded, then smiled. "Yes, sir."

"Just, stop calling him, 'sir'," Caitlin said. "I need you and Sorca both to help me out with giving this guy a hard time. It keeps him humble."

Nika let out a laugh, and even reached up to dab a finger against the corner of her eye. Buddy couldn't stand it. He reached over and pulled her against his chest.

"See?" he said. "What did I tell you? It's the season of miracles."

Caitlin tucked herself into Marq's side. He draped one arm across her shoulders.

"I guess the Department of Homeworld Security is getting another chef," she said.

"You already have one?" Buddy asked, keeping the conversation going both from curiosity and wanting to give Nika a chance to collect herself.

"We have two," Caitlin said. "And a barista. It's kind of weird, having that many foodies in the group responsible for Earth-alien relations."

Marq snorted. "If you'd spent your life eating nothing but nutrient bricks, you would understand why we hold your culinary engineers in such high regard."

"'Culinary engineer'," Buddy said. "Whoa, I like that."

Marq's expression faded back to that weird neutral state from before. "We can discuss the logistics when the mission is over, but for now, we have urgent matters to address."

"The Cygnians," Nika said.

Marq nodded. "We've dropped out of blue space. They should encounter us any moment."

As if on cue, a loud alarm sounded in the hallway.

"Any moment being now," Nika said.

Chapter Twelve

"Buddy, you have to get back to my quarters." Nika started tapping commands into her uniform's bracer. "I'll program the ship to show you the—"

"Coalition of Planets vessel." A booming voice filled the hall. "You have entered into Cygnian territory without invitation. Agree to be boarded, or be destroyed."

Oh shit.

Nika was pretty sure that was not how Marq wanted to start things off with the Cygnians. And how the heck were they projecting over the ship's internal communications system?

Pickles started barking, spinning in circles and looking around at the ceiling and walls. Buddy grabbed him—and Patches—holding them to his chest and shushing them.

Nika used her bracer to run a scan of the ship.

"Report," Marq said.

"They haven't breached our systems." Nika shook her head as she tried to make sense of the readings. "Somehow, they're creating a vibration in our hull and amplifying their voices. It's everywhere on the ship. How the hell are they doing that?"

"The Cygnians have their own tricks," Marq said. "There's a reason Cygnus X-3 is one of the only systems that wasn't brought into the Coalition—and it's not just because of the excessive gravity and radiation."

"Radiation?" Buddy clutched the animals closer to his chest. "Are we safe?"

"As long as we remain aboard, the ship will protect us," Nika said, wanting to reassure him.

"But if the Cygnians attack, the outcome is uncertain," Marq said.

Nika turned to face him. "You *had* to say that out loud?"

Marq ignored her glare. "The bridge is too far. We need to get to the auxiliary hangar bay. That's the safest place to greet them."

Marq started walking quickly down the hall, and the others followed.

If it came down to an attack, Nika knew Cyan would come to their aid. But she didn't want to tell Marq about the Vegan's presence unless she absolutely had to. Pissing off a Vegan to bring in the Cygnians was nowhere near an even trade.

"Wait, so you're just letting them come aboard?" Caitlin said.

"We can turn this to our advantage." Marq lifted his bracer and used it to open a communications channel. "Vay and Sorca, report to hangar bay three immediately."

He accessed a lift and stepped in as soon as the door had opened. Everyone filed in after him.

"Caitlin, you should take Buddy somewhere safe," Nika said.

"There is nowhere safe on the ship until we deal with this," Marq said.

"Again with the oversharing," Nika said.

"I'd rather know the truth." Buddy held the animals tight, his mouth a grim line and his brow furrowed.

"Besides, I'm not leaving Marq," Caitlin said.

"I need your full attention." Marq looked pointedly at Nika. "There's an observation room in the hangar where Buddy can await you."

"No way," Buddy said. "I'm not leaving Nika's side, either."

Marq sighed. "Then the *animals* can remain in the observation room."

It would have to do. Nika wanted to hold Buddy's hand, but didn't see how she could at the moment. She stepped closer instead, their arms brushing.

"I'm sorry, Buddy," she said.

He laughed. "Hey, I'm the one who stowed away in your truck."

"That's how you came aboard?" Caitlin asked.

Buddy shrugged. "I was going to surprise her with a Solstice dinner."

"Aww." Caitlin's smile faded into a frown. "Why'd you

bring your dog?"

"Pickles has a mind of his own," Buddy said. "He stowed away in the picnic basket."

Caitlin laughed. "I want to hear that entire story when this is done."

Nika was sure she was putting on a brave face, trying to keep things light. Everyone was on edge. The next few moments could turn the tide of the war.

The door to the lift opened onto the hangar bay and everyone hurried out. Nika led Buddy to the observation room.

He set Pickles down and said, "Stay." Then he lifted Patches and said, "You're the smart one. You have to keep him in here, okay? Where it's safe."

Patches let out a long meow.

"Don't give me that lip," Buddy said. "Pickles needs you. You guys are friends, and friends look out for each other, right?"

The kitten let out a little huffing breath. Nika was really starting to come around to Buddy's whole, "Patches is intelligent" argument.

"You can watch everything from the window." Nika pointed at the glass that separated the observation room from the rest of the hangar.

Great. Now I'm talking to her, too.

Patches jumped down from Buddy's arms, then up onto the counter in front of the window. Nika was still wrapping her head around that when Buddy grabbed her and drew her into a huge hug.

She held him for as long as she dared, but knew they were needed outside.

"Everything's going to be okay," she said. "It's the season of hope, remember?"

"Yeah." He cast a subdued smile at her. "Thanks."

That was as good as they were going to get. She nodded, then led him from the room.

Vay and Sorca had arrived by the time Nika and Buddy joined them. Eric was there as well. They were just opening a channel to the Cygnians. Vay was nodding vigorously at Marq, motioning with her hands for him to proceed.

"Cygnian vessel," Marq said. "I am Marq, commander of the *Reckoning*. We come to you with our weapons at our feet and our heads bowed. We do not seek battle on this day."

Nika held her breath as she waited for a response. This time, it came through the communications speaker. At least this part of the conversation wouldn't be broadcast to the entire crew.

"The *Reckoning* is a ship of war," the Cygnian said.

"Yes." Marq looked at Vay, who nodded and mouthed words to him that Nika couldn't understand. "We may meet in battle yet, but I hope it will be side-by-side."

"You can not add to our strength, *Sadirian*," the Cygnian said. "You know you can not best us. Victory will be ours."

Damn, this guy sounded just like Sorca. Which was a little weird, since Sorca had never had contact with an actual Cygnian before.

"Victories are hollow if your opponent will not fight," Marq said.

"You *will* fight," the Cygnian said.

Marq shook his head. "We will not."

There was another long pause before the Cygnian responded. "What is your designation?"

"I am Marq."

"What is your *designation*?" the Cygnian repeated.

Marq clenched his jaw. "I no longer answer to it."

A low chuckle rumbled over the speaker. "You turn your back on your people—your customs."

Vay started vigorously shaking her head. Marq gestured for her to calm down.

"I turn my back on the lies and betrayals of the High Council," Marq said. "I embrace my people and a new path forward. One that I hope will lead to friendship with the Cygnians."

Vay closed her eyes, her body practically vibrating with stress. She rose onto her toes and stayed there, not moving, not even breathing. Her hands were clenched together in front of her chest.

Sorca laughed, in typical Sorca fashion. All the reprogramming and clone bodies the High Council had subjected her to had really taken their toll on her personality.

But...did they?

"We do not seek your friendship," the Cygnian said. "We seek revenge. Make peace with your end."

Vay dropped back down on her heels, covering her mouth as she shook her head. Marq took Caitlin's hand in his.

"Cygnian coward," Sorca yelled.

A deafening roar sounded over the comm. "I am no coward!"

"Do you seek to kill your own kind?" Sorca said, her lips pulled back in a snarl.

They waited through the longest pause yet.

"Identify yourself." The Cygnian drew out the words, making each syllable a threat.

"I am Sorca," she said, mirroring his tone. "And the same DNA that made you is part of me."

"The construct," he said.

Nika bristled at the term. The High Council had treated Sorca like a replaceable object. Nika would be damned if she let the Cygnians do the same.

"The *friend*," Nika said. "And before you ask, I am Nika, chief engineer of the whole damn Coalition *fleet*. And if you want my designation, you can go fuck yourself."

Marq was staring at Nika with his jaw open. He mouthed, "What are you doing?"

Weird as she was, Sorca was Nika's closest friend. Nika

knew Sorca's quirks better than anyone—except Eric. And after listening to this guy, Nika was wondering if they really were quirks…or just part of her DNA.

The Cygnian started to laugh. He laughed for a long time. When he'd finally finished, he said, "I will meet you, chief engineer Nika. And I will see this 'Sorca' in the flesh. We board in five minutes."

The communication array beeped, letting them know he'd ended the transmission.

"What the hell was that?" Marq said.

"That was a victory." Sorca strode up to Nika and said, "And a well-earned one."

"Alliances aren't about one side or the other winning," Eric said. "They're about both sides winning."

"Then the first victory is ours." Sorca waved her hand dismissively. "They can have the next one."

Eric let out a long sigh.

"That went better than I expected," Vay said. "I mean, at least we didn't die."

"The night is young." Sorca smiled at her, showing too many teeth.

"Sorca," Eric said.

"Let her be." Nika stepped closer to Sorca, not quite matching her friend's smile. "Let her be…*Sorca*."

"What are you talking abou—" Marq cut off as Buddy shushed him.

"Hang on a minute," Buddy said. "She's piecing it all

together. She made the same face when she finally worked out how to fix my deep freeze."

Nika kept staring at Sorca, nose-to-nose.

"You have something to say?" Sorca cocked her head at Nika, still smiling, though without the feral glint.

"Everyone thinks of you as a Sadirian," Nika said.

Sorca shrugged. "That is the majority of my DNA."

"But is it the *victorious* DNA?" Nika said.

Sorca made the weirdest sound. Part laugh, part snarl, all…Sorca.

"You may look like a Sadirian, but I don't think you really are," Nika said. "I think you're Cygnian. Through-and-through. And every time you yell, 'victory' at the end of a staff-meeting, every time you accidentally knock somebody forward ten feet with a slap on the back, every single piece of equipment I've had to repair or replace because of your 'enthusiasm', I think your true nature is shining through."

Sorca's lips peeled from her teeth in the most feral smile Nika had ever seen. And that was saying something, after how much time they'd spent together.

Eric stepped forward. "You're suggesting that all the bloodlust and near-insane disregard for her own safety isn't because she always knew she had clone bodies to replace her, but..it's just part of being Cygnian?"

"We know the Cygnians are warriors," Nika said. "And that they value their traditions above all else."

"And now we think they're also super-impetuous and like…" Vay shook her head. "Really cocky?"

"*Crazy* cocky," Nika said.

"That's really not much to go on," Eric said. "How are we supposed to use that to win them over?"

"We don't." Marq locked his gaze with each person in turn. "If we really are going to try for an alliance, we're going to do it right. We do it with honesty."

Chapter Thirteen

Buddy felt absolutely useless. He wanted to pace. He wanted to throw something or kick something or just plain scream. But he didn't think the group of aliens around him would appreciate that.

Well, except maybe for the sorta-crazy one.

A loud beep sounded, along with some flashing lights. With a fizz-pop, a wall of staticy blue light came down between them and the main hangar area.

The far wall started to open.

On the other side was space, which was still freaking Buddy out. But not as much as the ship that hovered beyond.

It looked like a crystal—all sharp edges and smooth panes. The light caught and reflected off its milky-white surface, shining back in rainbows that filled the hangar. If Buddy wasn't so absolutely terrified of these guys, he would have thought it was beautiful.

When the door opened completely, the ship drifted in and landed on the hangar bay floor. More lights glinted across the surface of the ship as the outer door closed.

"Decontamination procedures," Nika said, suddenly at his side. "It takes care of stray radiation and any sort of contaminants that might be clinging to their hull."

"That's reassuring. Does it also take care of the near-invulnerable, impetuous, incredibly strong, and possibly angry-as-hell guys inside?"

Nika snorted, but even that was subdued. "They have reason to be angry, if they know what was done to Sorca."

The group had filled Buddy in on as much as they could in the limited time. And, yeah, Buddy would be pissed as hell, too, if he were them.

"But that wasn't you," he said. "That was the High Council."

"And all we have to do is convince the Cygnians of that."

The only thing keeping him from absolutely freaking out was remembering that there was a teeny, powerful lizard person on board. If she had to, Buddy was certain Cyan would help them. He hoped it wouldn't come to that, though.

Buddy pulled Nika close and kissed her. He soaked up as much of her warmth and love as he could. He didn't know when he'd get another chance.

"Guys," Caitlin said. "Seriously."

"And lose the hats." Eric nodded toward them.

Once again, Buddy had forgotten they were wearing them. He pulled his off and took Nika's when she handed it to him, then tucked them both into his belt.

So much for Christmas Cheer.

The decontamination lights went out and a moment after so did the flickering blue wall. Buddy felt a little light-headed, and realized he was holding his breath.

A hatch opened beneath the front of the ship and a ramp extended, hitting the floor with a dull thump.

"Any of you guys ever see a Cygnian before?" Buddy asked.

They responded with a chorus of "no".

Loud footsteps reverberated through the hangar. The first Cygnian appeared on the ramp, more of his body coming into view as he descended. The guy was *huge*. Bigger than a linebacker. But that wouldn't be what made him stand out in a crowd.

No, the shimmering silver-blue skin of his face and arms was the main eye-catcher. That, and his massive mane of blue hair. He had a beard to match. They all did. All *seven* of them.

Seven of them. Seven of us. But I do not like our odds.

Where Nika's people dressed in silver catsuits, these guys wore flat white leather tunics and matching pants. The light glinted off wide metal bracers on both of their wrists. As they approached, Buddy could make out that they each had eyes a different color of the rainbow. The vibrant colors almost seemed to glow.

Marq and Sorca stepped forward to greet them. Buddy's

heart felt like it lodged in his throat as Nika joined them.

The Cygnians stopped in front of the group. The man who'd exited the ship first leaned to the side, obviously sizing up Marq with his violet eyes. Tall as Marq was, the Cygnian still had half a foot on him. They must all be pushing seven feet.

"You are Marq," the Cygnian said.

Marq nodded. "I am."

The Cygnian turned to Nika and stepped close. Really close.

She didn't even flinch. Just jutted her chin and glared up at him. She was really playing up the cocky angle.

Buddy's chest flooded with warmth and pride. That was his woman. Fearless and strong.

Dammit, he wished he could stand beside her during this.

"You are Nika," the Cygnian said.

"Yeah," she said. "What of it?"

The Cygnian pulled his lips back from his teeth in a feral smile. "You suggested I 'go fuck myself'."

Nika stiffened.

"That was a strange command," the Cygnian said. "I am curious if our translators are functioning correctly."

"Okay, that's enough of that." Buddy stepped forward, insinuating himself between Nika and the towering blue dude. "That's an Earth expression and there's a lot to unpack with it. As one of the resident experts, I'd be happy to explain it to you."

The Cygnian straightened, then angled his head to the side as he stared at Buddy. "Who are you?"

"I'm Buddy."

What the hell am I doing?

The way Marq and the others had stiffened, they had to be wondering, too.

"Buddy of the sandwiches," Buddy said, digging the hole even deeper. "It's a kind of food. Anyway, I make a mean sub. You should try one some time."

"How can food be mean?" the Cygnian said.

"That…is…another thing that I will explain when you're done with the Sadirians. I mean talking with them," Buddy hastily added.

"You're not Sadirian?" the Cygnian asked.

"No, I'm an Earthling. From Earth." An Earthling who was in so far over his head, he didn't think he'd ever see the light of day again. "And who might you be?"

Buddy just imagined the whole group of Sadirians and Earthlings face-palming at his lame introduction. But if these guys were about swagger, there was no backing down now.

"I am Kral, son of Ehmach," the Cygnian said.

Vay let out a little "eep" noise. She cleared her throat, and said, "You're the crown prince of Cygnus-1."

Kral swung his head to face her, grinning. "Last I checked."

"It's an honor—" Vay scrunched her eyes and shook her head. "I mean… Go to hell!" Her eyes flew open and she clamped a hand over her mouth.

Kral just laughed. "Earth has joined the Coalition then. Strange, for such a primitive planet to be allowed the 'honor'." He filled the last word with an impressive amount of contempt.

"Earth has not joined with anyone," Eric said. "We have a tentative alliance with the Coalition of Planets—but only because their High Council has been…removed."

"Removed?" Kral laughed. All the Cygnians did. "Is that what you call getting your home system incinerated by the Tau Centaurans?"

Nika lunged forward, getting around Buddy. She stopped an inch away from Kral.

"Don't you dare," she said, between clenched teeth. "I was at that battle, and there was no glory in it. The Tau Centauran Assembly had tech that outstripped us by so far, we didn't even have a chance. That's not a victory. That's a slaughter."

The Cygnians' laughter stopped, but Kral was smiling. It was a normal smile this time.

Buddy was still holding his breath.

"Chief engineer Nika," Kral said. "Are you certain you aren't a warrior?"

"I'm a soldier," she said. "We're all warriors here."

Kral's lips peeled back in a smile again. He whipped his

head toward Sorca.

What was with this guy and the sudden head movements? Maybe it was a Cygnian thing.

He strode toward Sorca, his chest growing bigger as he took in a huge breath.

"But none is as great a warrior as Sorca," he said.

"I welcome any challenge." She looked up at him with a smile as feral as his own.

Vay leaned forward and said, "But you should know she's already bonded. So, if you want to fight, it's just for funsies."

Eric and Marq both turned to stare at her. Vay just shrugged.

"And what warrior could possibly have defeated you in battle?" Kral said.

"That would be me." Eric stepped forward.

"You?" Kral laughed. "How Cygnian are you, Sorca, that you were bested by an Earthling?"

Sorca smiled. Almost faster than Buddy could see, she dropped into a crouch, then lunged forward, catching Kral at his waist. She lifted him from the ground, holding the guy who was easily twice her size in the air as if it was nothing.

"Sorca," Eric snapped. Sorca was positioning her hands on Kral's chest and thigh, like she was getting ready to toss him.

"If you could put him down, please," Marq said.

She set Kral back on his feet and smoothed his tunic where she'd grabbed him. "I am Cygnian enough."

Kral laughed as he grabbed Sorca and picked her up. Her feet dangled and flailed as he hugged her.

"You are," Kral said. "Of course you are."

"Put me down, or I'll gut you," she said.

Kral laughed even harder, but he did as she asked. He kept one hand on her shoulder and lifted her chin with the other.

"The Assembly told us you had been destroyed, along with the *copies* the High Council made of you," Kral said.

Sorca bared her teeth again in something not even close to a smile. "I am not so easily killed."

Kral nodded. "No, you are not."

"So, does this mean you're not going to kill us?" Buddy said.

Kral clasped Sorca to his side and grinned. "Not today."

"That's…reassuring, I guess," Buddy said.

"We hope this is the beginning of a closer relationship between our people," Marq said.

Kral shook his head, his smile fading. "There will be no closeness."

"But—" Vay stopped when Kral cut her off with a gesture.

"We have our own ways," Kral said. "And we will not change."

"The High Council were the ones who insisted upon a

monolithic culture," Marq said. "They professed to seek peace through uniformity. But they are gone, and the Coalition has changed."

"And now that you allow variation of customs among your people, how will you manage peace?" Kral said. "How will you teach septillions of sentients how to interact with each other when they have all been forced to agree on everything for so long?"

"We're figuring it out," Marq said.

"The Cygnians have our own ways," Kral said. "We are a passionate and volatile people."

Buddy shrugged. "Isn't everybody?"

"Not everyone is hardy enough to handle us," Kral said.

"We might surprise you," Buddy said.

Kral smiled at him, then spun around and grabbed one of the Cygnians behind him by the front of his tunic. He flung the guy twenty feet across the hangar. Right at the window to the observation room.

The glass shattered into pebbles when the guy hit it. It was like he was made out of rock. He kept going, bouncing off the wall hard enough to leave a dent in it before falling to the ground.

Everybody in the silver catsuits started to lift their arms, hands poised over their bracers to…do something helpful, presumably. Buddy lifted his arm, mimicking them, even though he had no idea what he was doing. Honestly, he thought they were about to get their asses handed to them.

But the Cygnians just laughed. All of them. Even the guy who'd been flung through the window was laughing when he rose.

He lifted an arm, and said, "Look at this thing that's biting me."

Pickles was hanging from his sleeve, teeth dug in and head twisting as he thrashed from side to side.

"Pickles!" Buddy ran toward the room. "That's my dog!"

"Be careful with that…whatever it is," Kral said.

Patches leapt up onto the counter, then down to the floor of the hangar bay. Neither she nor Pickles seemed hurt, thankfully.

The kitten ran over to Marq and climbed up to sit on his shoulder again. Pickles released his grip on the Cygnian, then hopped onto the counter and through the open window into the hangar bay.

Instead of running to Buddy, the teeny dog charged Kral, barking like crazy. Pickles bit Kral's boot and started shaking his head back and forth again.

Kral looked down at Pickles, no longer laughing. His gaze snapped to Buddy.

"What is this thing?" Kral said.

"That's my dog." Buddy ran over and tried to pull Pickles off the guy. "Sorry about that. He probably thinks you're a threat. Aw, Pickles, no!"

Pickles squirmed out of Buddy's grip and jumped up at

Kral again, growling and barking fiercely. Kral raised one eyebrow at Buddy, then reached down toward the dog.

"Careful," Buddy yelled. "Dogs are delicate. At least the teeny ones."

"Somebody should tell him that." Kral laughed as Pickles lit into the Cygnian's hands and arms, biting away —and not bothering Kral one bit, from the look of things. "You are a *fierce* one," Kral said, holding Pickles close and standing.

He froze, an odd expression on his face.

"What… What is this?" Kral said.

"I keep telling you, that's my dog," Buddy said. "It's an Earth creature. A pet."

"It's so soft." Kral turned to the others and held Pickles up for them to pet.

The Cygnians all gasped when they touched Pickles's fur, passing him around and gently petting him. Pickles whined, obviously torn between teaching these guys a lesson and basking in the attention.

"I'm guessing you guys don't have fuzzy animals on…" Buddy tried to remember the name of their planet, but just settled on, "your homeworld."

"Our planet is made almost entirely of rock and crystal," Kral said. "The softest thing we have is our leathers."

He hooked his thumb in his vest and leaned forward for Buddy to feel.

Okay, this is…strange…

Buddy didn't want to offend the guy, so he felt the fabric and almost immediately recoiled.

"Oh my God," he said. "That's like…the worst wool sweater I ever wore times a thousand. It's one step up from sandpaper."

Kral nodded, then turned to the others. "Give me back the dog."

Pickles settled in Kral's arms, and even reached up and gave him a few hesitant chin-licks.

Kral held perfectly still, but his eyebrows lowered. "What is it doing now?"

"Those are dog kisses," Buddy said. "Highly sought after on Earth."

Kral arched an eyebrow, but said nothing.

"So, this is progress." Vay stepped forward. "Sure, there are some blips to work out, but I know we can find a way to work together."

"You saw what happened just now," Kral said. "Your environments can't even stand up to us. We constantly practice with each other for battle. What happens when we forget ourselves and strike one of you too hard?" Kral shook his head. "It's too great a risk. We can not change our ways. We are what we are."

Buddy laughed. When everyone looked at him, he shrugged.

"Hey, when I was a kid, I used to fight all the time." He pointed at the bend in his nose, then toward his side.

"Broken nose. Broken ribs."

"So, you often lost," Kral said.

Buddy laughed again. "You should've seen the other guys."

Kral's mouth pulled into a feral grin.

"But I had people counting on me," Buddy said. "My parents. My sisters. I knew I had to learn to control myself. So I channeled my temper into making bread. I have a bad day, I let it out on the dough. I got so much practice, people started paying me for what I baked. I put all that energy into my sandwiches, and made a life out of it."

"You're saying...we should make sandwiches?" Kral said.

"No, not sandwiches." Buddy shook his head. "You have to find your own thing."

"Our custom is to fight," Kral said.

"Okay." Buddy shrugged. "So, fight each other. Let loose then. But when you're around others, be careful. Find another way to be together and enjoy each others' company."

Kral shook his head. "That isn't our way."

"Aren't you the prince?" Buddy said. "You can't tell your people to try something new? Or better yet, you can show them."

Chapter Fourteen

Nika loved where Buddy was going with this. She came to stand at his side, and said, "You're already trying something new."

Kral raised an eyebrow at her.

She pointed at Pickles. "Look how gentle you're being with Buddy's dog. If you hadn't tried to hold him—if you hadn't been careful—you would have missed out on a new experience."

"A warrior does not shy away from battle," Sorca said. "Even if their opponent is themselves."

"You are saying this because you seek an alliance," Kral said. "We are too different to ally with anyone. Our ways, our forms, are set, like the crystal of our planet."

Nika shook her head. "Crystals *can* grow. We're not saying all this to get an alliance. We're saying this because it's true. Trying new things can lead to amazing experiences. Like..." She turned to Buddy and said, "Buddy, tell them about the Solstice celebration you had planned for me."

"What? Oh, okay." He thought for a moment, then said,

"Where I was born, when Winter comes around, the days are short and the nights long. It gets cold and dark and the plants all die and most of the trees lose their leaves."

"And you celebrate this?" Kral said.

Buddy laughed. "No, that's not what we celebrate. We celebrate each other. We share food and stories, and…really just each other's company. There's lights and music and all the best parts of being human. We have all kinds of different holidays this time of year that mean different things to different people. But the one thing we all have in common is that we're with the people we love."

"I do not understand this tradition," Kral said.

"There's a lot to it," Nika said. "Everybody celebrates in their own way, but that actually makes the season more special."

"There is no unity," Kral said. "A lack of unity leads to discord."

Buddy shook his head. "No, no, no. You have it all wrong. With all the variety we have on Earth, we can achieve something we'd never be able to if we were all… singing the same note."

"Which is?"

"Harmony," Buddy said, and smiled. "Sure, we struggle and we fight sometimes. But we also bring ourselves together in the most beautiful ways. It's like…"

Buddy snapped his fingers, then pointed toward Nika. "Can we call my family from here?"

Nika's eyebrows hiked up her forehead. Her idea was starting to get away from her.

"You want me to open a communication channel to Earth?" she asked.

Buddy nodded. "Yeah. To my family. I need to talk to them."

"Buddy, it's okay." She took his hand in hers and interlaced their fingers. "We're going to get you back to Earth."

"I know that." Buddy laughed. "What, do you think I don't have faith in you? I know you're going to get us back to Earth. But I want to make a difference while I'm here. Please, let me help."

Nika glanced over at Marq, who nodded. She released Buddy's hand and activated a comm channel through her bracer, using the numbers Buddy told her to establish a connection.

It only took a few moments for a woman's voice to sound through the hangar.

"Buddy, is that you?" she said.

"Yeah, Mom." Buddy pinched the bridge of his nose and shut his eyes.

After hearing more about this holiday and what it meant, Nika understood how much he must be missing his family.

"I've been worried sick," his mom said. "Where are you? You're not answering calls or texts or email. It's Christmas Eve!"

"Mom, listen," he said. "Nika had…a family emergency. It's really serious. I'm with her right now."

"Oh no!" His mom's tone switched from admonishing to sympathetic instantly. "Oh, tell her we're thinking about her."

"I will."

"Darn, I was really hoping to meet her," his mom said. "The first woman my boy ever asked to bring home for Christmas!"

He cringed, and said, "Can we maybe talk about that later?"

"Sure, sweetie."

"I was hoping you could do me a favor," Buddy said.

"Anything. How can we help?"

Nika felt as if she'd been struck in the chest. This woman that she hadn't even met was so ready to help her. Nika knew she loved Buddy. But now, she was starting to love his family, too.

"Can you have the girls sing my favorite Christmas song?" Buddy looked over at Kral, then to Nika. "I want to share our tradition with Nika's family. Something new for them to enjoy. To help them feel better."

"What a great idea," his mom said. "Hang on."

Nika heard her yell, "Girls!" really loud in the background. She bit her lips to keep from laughing.

There was more chatter, and several voices joined in. One voice came through clearly, a lot younger than the first.

"You are so dead, Buddy," she said. "Missing Christmas to be with your girlfriend? Lame."

Kral cocked his head to the side.

"That's my sister Becca," Buddy said. "She's a real sweetheart. And doesn't know we're already on speaker phone."

"Oh shit," Becca said. "Sorry."

In the background, Nika heard Buddy's mom yell, "Language!"

Buddy just shook his head. He shrugged, and said, "Family. You know?"

"Does that mean I get to be the first to talk to her?" Becca asked.

"She isn't really..." Buddy sighed. "We're not in a place where she can talk. It's hard to explain, but—"

"It's okay," Becca said. "I'm just giving you a hard time, and I shouldn't be. Sorry."

"Look at that," Buddy said. "It's a Christmas miracle."

Becca snorted. "Shut up. Just let her know I hope everything ends up okay."

"Why are we singing early?" Another young woman's voice spoke up in the background.

"Nika's family needs the comfort," his mom said. "It's okay to break tradition to help people out. Now be quiet and sing."

There was a pause, then they all started laughing. That

sound in itself was beautiful to Nika's ears.

If everything worked out with Buddy, this would be her family some day. And she wanted that so badly, she could hardly stand it.

She looked over at Kral and the Cygnians. They had formed a semi-circle around Buddy and Nika and were listening intently. At least they were giving this a shot. Whatever "this" was.

"You all ready there?" Buddy's mom said.

"Yeah, Mom."

"Okay, here we go."

There was a humming sound—sustained voices holding the same note—and then one by one, each voice began singing a different but complimentary melody. The way they combined and synchronized with each other, they created harmonic convergences that made her breath catch in her throat and the hair on her arms stand on end.

Nika looked around to see if the others were having a similar reaction to the sweet words and heart-felt melody. Buddy had a soft smile on his face and a far-off look in his eye. Marq and Caitlin were standing with their arms around each other. Even Eric and Sorca were holding hands. Vay stood with her eyes closed, listening intently.

The Cygnians... The Cygnians stood ramrod straight, their eyes glowing and faces upturned.

Nika felt a vibration through the floor. She looked over at the Cygnian ship and saw light shimmer over its crystalline surface. The harmonics of the sound were being caught and magnified, transmitted through the ship, just like their earlier communication.

Kral curled his free hand into a fist and pressed it against his chest near his shoulders. He lifted Pickles to the same spot on the other side, seemingly oblivious to the dog licking his chin. Kral's jaw was clenched, a muscle standing out in his cheek above his beard.

The song wound down, with Buddy's sisters all sustaining long notes that bolstered each other in the most perfect harmony that Nika had ever experienced. The vibration beneath her feet ended along with the song.

There was a moment of silence, then Buddy's mom said, "Oh, girls. That was lovely."

Buddy cleared his throat and said, "I love you, Mom."

His mom laughed. "I love you, too, Buddy. We all do."

One of the sisters—Becca?—said, "Meh. He's okay. Nika could probably do better."

Nika clapped a hand over her mouth to mask the laugh she could barely stop.

"Merry Christmas, sweetie," his mom said. The others piped in with a chorus of, "Merry Christmas."

"Merry Christmas, everybody," Buddy said.

His mom suddenly added, "Oh, wait! Tell Nika Happy Solstice! That's what her family celebrates, right?"

"I'll tell her," Buddy said. "Bye."

"Bye, son."

Nika tapped on her bracer to end the transmission.

Everyone stood in silence for a long time. Pickles whined, then leaned up and licked Kral's chin again. The Cygnian patted the dog absently, pacing a few steps away from his fellows.

"Earth does not have a monolithic culture," he said, his voice a bit coarser than before.

"Monolithic?" Buddy asked. "You mean, we're all different on Earth? Yeah, I guess so. We do our thing. Live and let live, for the most part. We have our difficulties, but we're working through them. Just like Marq says the Coalition is doing."

"They have no idea what they're doing," Kral said.

"Give us a chance, and we might surprise you," Nika said.

Kral smiled at her. "Of that, I have no doubt."

He shook his head and took a few more steps away from his group, drawing closer to Buddy.

"I have made my decision," Kral said. "With full authorization of my father."

Nerves flared up in Nika's stomach, like sparks from a severed power cable.

"We will not ally ourselves with the Coalition," Kral said.

Nika was in free-fall. It was like the artificial gravity generators had failed. If the Cygnians sided with the Tau Centaurans, they were screwed.

"We will not ally ourselves with the Tau Centauran Assembly, either," Kral said.

That's good at least.

Their mission was damage control, and at least they'd managed that. Still, she had thought they would side with the Coalition. She had felt...hope.

Kral closed the distance between himself and Buddy, then reached out and clasped Buddy's shoulder, still holding Pickles with his other hand.

"The Cygnians choose to ally ourselves with Earth," Kral said.

Chapter Fifteen

Buddy wasn't sure he'd heard Kral right. Did he say they were allying with…Earth?

Holy shit. Did I just negotiate an alliance with a bunch of aliens using a Christmas song and four-part harmony?

"How long do you need to prepare for our arrival?" Kral said.

"Well, I don't know how long it'll take us to get back, and my mom didn't really expect so much company, but—" Buddy shook himself. "Wait, what now?"

"If we are to be allies, we must understand your ways," Kral said. "And I am most interested in learning how so many cultures coexist on one small planet."

"I… Well…" Buddy stammered. "My place isn't that big."

Nika came up behind him and wrapped her arms around his waist. "Don't worry, Buddy. As Earth's other allies, we'd be happy to help you construct a site worthy of the Cygnians' presence." She smiled up at Kral. "With very sturdy walls."

Kral's face split in a huge grin. "And more of those

sound waves. What is it called?" He turned back to Buddy.

"You mean music?" Buddy said.

"Music," Kral repeated. "It is most excellent. Soft and powerful. Like your dog." He lifted Pickles a bit and laughed.

"Music is a huge part of Earth's various cultures," Nika said. "There's actually a huge variety of—"

Buddy reached out and took her hand in his. "Maybe let's stick with the sweet, calming stuff before we bring out the heavy metal."

Nika's favorite music could wake the dead. If his sisters' singing had had such a profound effect on Kral and the other Cygnians, Buddy didn't want to think of what heavy metal could do.

Okay, actually, that might be kind of fun—from a safe distance—but he'd save it for after they'd had some practice keeping their "passion and volatility" under control.

"Earth has such potential," Kral said. "There are many sentients you can aid by sharing your wisdom and accomplishments."

Buddy felt his eyebrows hike up on his forehead. These aliens, with all their advanced technology, were looking to *Earth* to figure out how to live?

Just one more miracle to be grateful for. And something to strive toward being worthy of.

"Before we leave, I would like to learn more about these

Earth holidays your mother mentioned," Kral said.

Vay clapped her hands together. "I actually have a room all prepared with half a dozen different winter celebrations."

"Half a dozen?" Kral asked.

"Oh, yes," she said. "I think you'll be amazed by Earth. It's home to the most diversified culture we've ever encountered."

"Here." Buddy pulled the red hats from his belt and tossed them to Vay. "This is…traditional Christmas attire."

"Santa hats!" Vay exclaimed.

Her smile broadened as she handed Kral a hat and put her own on. Kral arched an eyebrow, but tugged his on as well.

"Vay is our cultural liaison," Marq said. "She's been studying Earth for months and is our resident expert. Aside from the Earthlings themselves, of course."

"Aww, thanks." Caitlin rested her head on Marq's chest.

"Then lead on," Kral said, gesturing forward with Pickles.

"Um, about my dog?" Buddy said.

"I will keep him safe," Kral said.

"Yeah, but—"

"*I* will keep him safe." Caitlin smiled at Buddy, then followed everyone else out of the room, leaving Buddy and Nika alone.

"Pickles will be a great bridge between all of our

people," Nika said, her tone so serious, she had to be making a joke.

And yet...

"Great," Buddy said. "My dog, the ambassador for Earth."

"You make a good team." She shifted to stand in front of him, placing her arms around his neck.

"*We* make a good team." He rested his hands on her hips.

"We do," she said. "So, am I really the only woman you've ever planned to take home to meet your family?"

He smiled. "Like I said before, you are my family."

Before she could say anything else, he leaned in and kissed her. And then, nothing more needed to be said.

Epilogue

Six months, nineteen days, and twenty-two hours. That was how long Kral had to wait to set foot on Earth.

As his craft descended through the atmosphere, he watched the lights of the cities fill the viewports—clusters and streams of gold that glittered like stars on the surface of their planet.

There was only one light that truly interested him, though. The light at Buddy's mother's house. The light that led to Becca.

Kral lifted his fists to his hearts again, remembering how her voice had lit up every cell in his body, causing his hearts to beat in sequence. He had never experienced anything like it before.

Unfortunately, before he sought out Becca, he needed to make his appearance at the town the Department of Homeworld Security had created for him and for other aliens visiting their world.

If they were truly to learn how to coexist, as the Earthlings did, Kral doubted their lessons would come from just this town. He wanted to see the world, interact with the humans living there. Learn from them.

Maybe get a dog.

His ship hovered over an airstrip, then floated to one of several large hangars designed to look like regular Earth buildings. As soon as they had touched down inside, the hangar doors closed.

Kral stood and turned to his spectrum of warriors. "Remember, treat everything and everyone on this planet as if it's made of fledgling crystal."

The others nodded.

With that distraction addressed, he turned his thoughts to his purpose. Strengthening the alliance with Earth, yes. But more than that.

To find the Earthling Becca. To learn the meaning of how her voice stirred him so.

The Sadirian called Vay awaited them in the bright lights from the lamps above the door to the hangar bay. She smiled broadly, bouncing up on her toes as he approached.

"Welcome to Harbor," she said. "I think you'll enjoy your stay."

—

The Department of Homeworld Security series is heading in an exciting new direction! I can't wait to see what happens in the new town of Harbor, Kansas. And I'm sure we're going to see some adventures on those colonies Nika is building in the Sol system. Why, there might even be a new spin-off series in the works (or two... or three)! Be sure to join my newsletter so you don't miss anything! In the meantime, we're heading back to Harbor for a new adventure. Read on for an excerpt!

Nothing to Declare

The Department of Homeworld Security
Book Thirteen

Chapter One

"There is something wrong with me."

Sabrina shook her head as she steered around the last corner before the "Look Again Pet Parlor" building. How had she managed to get through her entire evening without realizing she'd left her phone at work?

She wasn't sure which was worse—that she hadn't noticed her phone was gone or that she felt compelled to retrieve it before finally getting some sleep. Her body made its opinion clear as she let out a long yawn.

She could have waited till morning to get her phone, but that would mean she couldn't be reached quickly in case of an emergency. People were counting on her to keep their pets safe and happy.

Harbor wasn't a big town, but she and her best friend, Kimmy, had worked hard to make a name for themselves in the surrounding counties. They were the best groomer and boarding facility for hundreds of miles. Miles that were mostly farmland dotted with other tiny towns, but still…

With the Winter Fair only a few days behind them, Sabrina's fingers were still stiff from plaiting the manes of a dozen horses in intricate designs with festive garlands woven in.

That was Kimmy's brilliant idea to drum up business. Show off how pretty they could make people's animals and raise enough money to expand their building. Then they could have individual pet rooms for the animals to stay in instead of their current kennels. Sabrina was all for that.

And the thing was, it had worked. There had been a huge influx of customers since the fair ended. Kimmy was thriving on it. Sabrina was starting to drag.

If it would help them provide a better home-away-from-home for the animals, she'd get through it, though. And at least she'd be able to jump right into bed when she got home. She was already in her pajamas under her coat—the thick fleece matching set covered in rainbows and unicorns.

She turned off her headlights before pulling into the farthest spot from the door, not wanting to disturb the current boarders any more than was necessary. It was bad enough they'd be hearing her car engine.

Maybe she'd just sleep in the office tonight. Again. There was a cot set up for her and everything. It was uncomfortable as heck, but she usually felt better staying near the pets she was caring for.

They only had two dogs with them at the moment, but they also had seven cats. Mrs. Simpkins had brought in her entire menagerie—named after the seven dwarves—while her house was being fumigated.

Sabrina tucked a few stray blond strands under her bright purple stocking cap as she stepped into the brisk air. The Winter had been comparatively mild, but it was still cold as heck this late at night.

She closed her car door as quietly as she could, then used her key to slip in the back door of the building. Her keys clinked loudly as she dropped them into her purse and she froze, eyes closed as she waited for the barking to start.

Nobody made a sound.

She shut the door, slowly moving deeper into the building. A shiver ran down her spine that had nothing to do with the chill air that had followed her inside. It took her overtaxed brain a moment to realize what was wrong—aside from the eerie silence.

There was a light moving around in the kennel room. She could see it through the frosted glass window on the door.

Sabrina had locked up after a final check on the animals. No one else should be there.

Kimmy might have come back to do some late night paperwork. Or maybe she'd forgotten her phone, too. But she would have turned on the lights to see better.

No. Someone had broken in and was… Doing what? Robbing the dogs? Stealing the cat toys?

Sabrina needed to call Sheriff Mariana. But the shop didn't have a landline, and her phone was probably in the room with whoever that was. She always spent the last part of her shift with their guests to make sure they were settled for the night.

What would anybody want with a tiny pet parlor in a town so small she could walk from one end to the other in twenty minutes? It didn't make sense for it to be a thief. But then, who else could it be?

It was probably some kind of prank from the local high schoolers. There was nothing else to do in Harbor.

Sabrina crept closer to the door, determined to surprise the kids and give them hell for whatever hijinks they were up to.

"You're sure this won't hurt them?" a man said.

Sabrina would have enjoyed the low timbre and richness of his voice if his words hadn't sent another chill down her spine.

"Of course it will not." The second voice was higher pitched and had a strange sibilance to it. "Now stop distracting me and let us continue our work."

Not high schoolers…

Sabrina's heartbeat picked up. Someone really had broken in. And they were doing something that might hurt the animals.

Was that why she hadn't heard any barking? Had they already done something to the dogs?

Rage overwhelmed her fear. She stuck her hand in her purse and pulled out her stun-gun, suddenly glad she'd given in to her grandpa's insistence that she always carry one, even in the small, "safe" town. Before she could talk herself out of it, she opened the door to the kennels, flicking the light switch on as she burst into the room.

"Don't move," she shouted, blinking against the sudden brightness.

The man inside was having a similar issue with the light. He held one hand high, shielding his eyes.

As he lowered his arm, he said, "I thought you were running active scans so we wouldn't be surprised."

Sabrina looked all around the room. Pancakes and Fluffy were sitting up in their kennels, mouths open in broad smiles and tails wagging as they looked at her from under the carefully styled white fur that dangled from their foreheads.

Not a hair on their furry little bodies seemed to be out of place. They even still had their bows on.

The cat kennels seemed as full as they'd been when Sabrina left. It was hard to count all the occupants while she was trying to keep watch on the intruder and...

Where was his accomplice? Sabrina had heard two distinct voices, but only saw the one guy.

The one super-hot guy.

He had short, light-brown hair and dark blue eyes with crinkles at the edges, as if he laughed a lot. His jaw was cut, his features strong—as well as his physique. She could see a lot of it, since he was just wearing a gray T-shirt that had a green design around the collar, and khakis, with what looked like boat shoes.

Doesn't this guy know it's Winter?

Movement on his broad shoulders brought her attention back up from his seasonally inappropriate outfit. She almost screamed as what she'd thought was a colorful design on his shirt collar lifted its head and flicked its long tail.

He had an iguana on his shoulders.

The biggest iguana she had ever seen. It had to be at least three feet long without counting its tail.

What the heck kind of burglar brought his pet lizard along with him when he broke into a grooming and boarding shop?

"We can explain," the guy said.

Another chill shivered down her spine at the reminder that he wasn't alone—and she wasn't thinking about the iguana. Sabrina quickly shifted to have her back to the wall. She kept one eye on the door so no one could sneak up on her.

"Where's your accomplice?" Sabrina demanded.

"Accomplice? I don't know what you mean."

"You were talking to someone a minute ago. Where are they?"

He looked over at the iguana. The exhaustion must really be taking its toll, because Sabrina almost thought the iguana looked back at him. Like a meaningful exchange was taking place.

"Look, this is all a misunderstanding," he said. "My name is Len and this is Cyan."

He gestured to the lizard as he took a step forward, but froze when Sabrina lifted her stun-gun higher. His gaze locked on it as if he hadn't noticed it before.

"Wait... Is that a projectile weapon?" His voice had risen and his eyes were wide.

"Projectile? You mean like bullets?" She shook her head. "It's a stun-gun."

Stop reassuring the bad guy, Sabrina!

Dang it, she really had to watch that. She quickly added, "It'll electrocute you if I shoot you with it, so don't try anything."

"Electrocute me?" His eyebrows rose. "That's insane."

"Insane? You're the one who broke into my shop and brought along your pet lizard."

The iguana narrowed its eyes and let out a loud hiss. Sabrina instinctively pointed her stun-gun at it, then realized Len was the bigger threat and brought it back to her first target.

"First of all, Cyan is not my pet," he said. "She's my friend."

Sabrina shook her head. This guy was sounding crazier by the moment.

"That does nothing to explain what you're doing here in the middle of the night messing with my boarders," Sabrina said.

"Boarders?"

The iguana let out a series of hisses, pops, and clicks. Sabrina didn't know they were so vocal. Len nodded and then shrugged.

"Oh, the animals," he said. "Why do they call them 'boarders', though?"

Sabrina blinked a few times as she tried to come up with an explanation for how he was interacting with his pet. The only one that seem feasible was also completely ridiculous.

He was talking to the iguana. And pretending—or imagining—that the iguana was talking back.

"I'm calling the police," Sabrina said.

Except she still didn't have her phone. She didn't see it anywhere.

Even more disconcerting, she still didn't see the woman he'd been talking to earlier. Unless he'd been talking to himself and just making up the other voice.

That was too creepy to think about.

Maybe the voice had come from the iguana.

She barely kept herself from laughing at the thought.

No more overtime. The first thing she was doing after getting out of this encounter was calling Kimmy and insisting on taking a few days off.

"There's no need to call the police," Len said. "We'll leave."

"Not until you explain what you're doing here in the first place."

He let out a huge sigh. "We're aliens."

Sabrina did laugh that time. The sound almost drowned out the litany of hisses, clicks, and grumbles from the lizard.

"Only in Harbor," Sabrina said. "Okay, look, *tourist*. You need to do better research. Harbor doesn't have the most alien encounters or even alien sightings. It has the most crackpots who tell stories about them."

Her face heated at too many memories to process. She berated herself for using the word "crackpot".

Not. Cool. Sabrina.

"Nothing has ever been verified," she went on. "For those of us who live here, it's a town joke. And you're sure as hell playing to the wrong audience with me."

"Crackpots?" He cocked his head to the side.

Of course, he would zero in on that word. Sabrina felt her face heat even more, her skin prickling and her arms twitching with the urge to hit something.

On cue, the lizard hissed and clicked, as if she was explaining it to him. How had he trained it so well?

"That's not a very nice word," Len said.

Something zinged in her chest—in a not-unpleasant way. She deepened her scowl to fight it off.

"The guy who broke into my shop and was talking about hurting my cats does not get to critique my choice of words," she said.

"We aren't going to hurt anyone. We just need some DNA samples."

"DNA samples."

"Yes." He took a step forward, but again stopped when she raised the stun-gun higher. "A litter of kittens was recently born aboard one of our spaceships. They're exhibiting behavior that the Earthlings among us find unusual."

"The Earthlings. Right." Crazy as he was, the guy could spin a good story. "What kind of 'unusual behavior' are they exhibiting? Walking around on their back legs wearing a hat and a pair of boots?"

"Um, no. As limited as our experience is with this kind of life form, even we would have realized that was outside the norm. These cats are smart. Incredibly smart. They may have even sabotaged parts of the ship."

"Why would they do that?"

"To get the Chief Engineer's attention." He shrugged at her quizzical look. "Patches has a soft spot for her."

"Patches," Sabrina said. "And she's one of the super-intelligent space cats."

"Exactly. We need DNA samples from cats born on Earth—preferably a variety of them—to compare and use as a control group to see if there's been some sort of mutation with the cats on our ship."

"This is insane." She shook her head, trying to not get swept up in his story...with limited success. "Why come here?"

"Craig told us about the town, and when we learned about Marvin—"

All the rage from earlier when she'd thought he was threatening the cats crashed back into her, bringing along a slew of its friends.

Indignation. Frustration. And above all else, love.

Nobody messed with her family.

Sabrina pressed the trigger without consciously thinking about it. The darts flew out from the gun, striking the guy in the chest.

"Don't you dare bring my grandpa into this," Sabrina said.

Very consciously, she held down the button to deliver the charge.

—

About the Author

USA Today Bestselling author Cassandra Chandler uses her vivid imagination to make the world more interesting, spawning the ideas she turns into her whimsical Science Fiction romcoms and darkly evocative Paranormal and Urban Fantasy Romances. Fast-paced and funny, lighthearted or dark, her stories will introduce you to characters you want to be friends with and worlds where you'd like to build a vacation home.